Smokescreen

A Fernando Lopez Santa Fe Mystery

SMOKESCREEN

A FERNANDO LOPEZ SANTA FE MYSTERY

JAMES C. WILSON

Sunstone books may be purchased for educational, business, or sales promotional use.
For information please write: Special Markets Department, Sunstone Press,
P.O. Box 2321, Santa Fe, New Mexico 87504-2321.

Book and cover design › R. Ahl

eBook 978-1-61139-600-3

Library of Congress Cataloging-in-Publication Data

Names: Wilson, James C., 1948- author. | Wilson, James C., 1948- Fernando Lopez Santa Fe mystery ; 2.
Title: Smokescreen / by James C. Wilson.
Description: Santa Fe, New Mexico : Sunstone Press, [2021] | Series: A Fernando Lopez Santa Fe mystery | Summary: "When a prominent Santa Fe City Council member is assassinated at the annual Santa Fe Fiesta, Detective Fernando Lopez must negotiate cultural and ethnic conflicts to find his killer and expose his involvement in a sex-trafficking ring"-- Provided by publisher.
Identifiers: LCCN 2020047636 | ISBN 9781632933157 (paperback) | ISBN 9781611396188 (epub) | ISBN 9781632934017 (hardcover)
Subjects: LCSH: Lopez, Fernando (Fictitious character) | Murder--Investigation--New Mexico--Santa Fe--Fiction. | Human trafficking--Investigation--New Mexico--Santa Fe--Fiction. | LCGFT: Detective and mystery fiction.
Classification: LCC PS3623.I58485 S66 2021 | DDC 813/.6--dc23
LC record available at https://lccn.loc.gov/2020047636

WWW.SUNSTONEPRESS.COM
SUNSTONE PRESS / POST OFFICE BOX 2321 / SANTA FE, NM 87504-2321 /USA
(505) 988-4418 / FAX (505) 988-1025

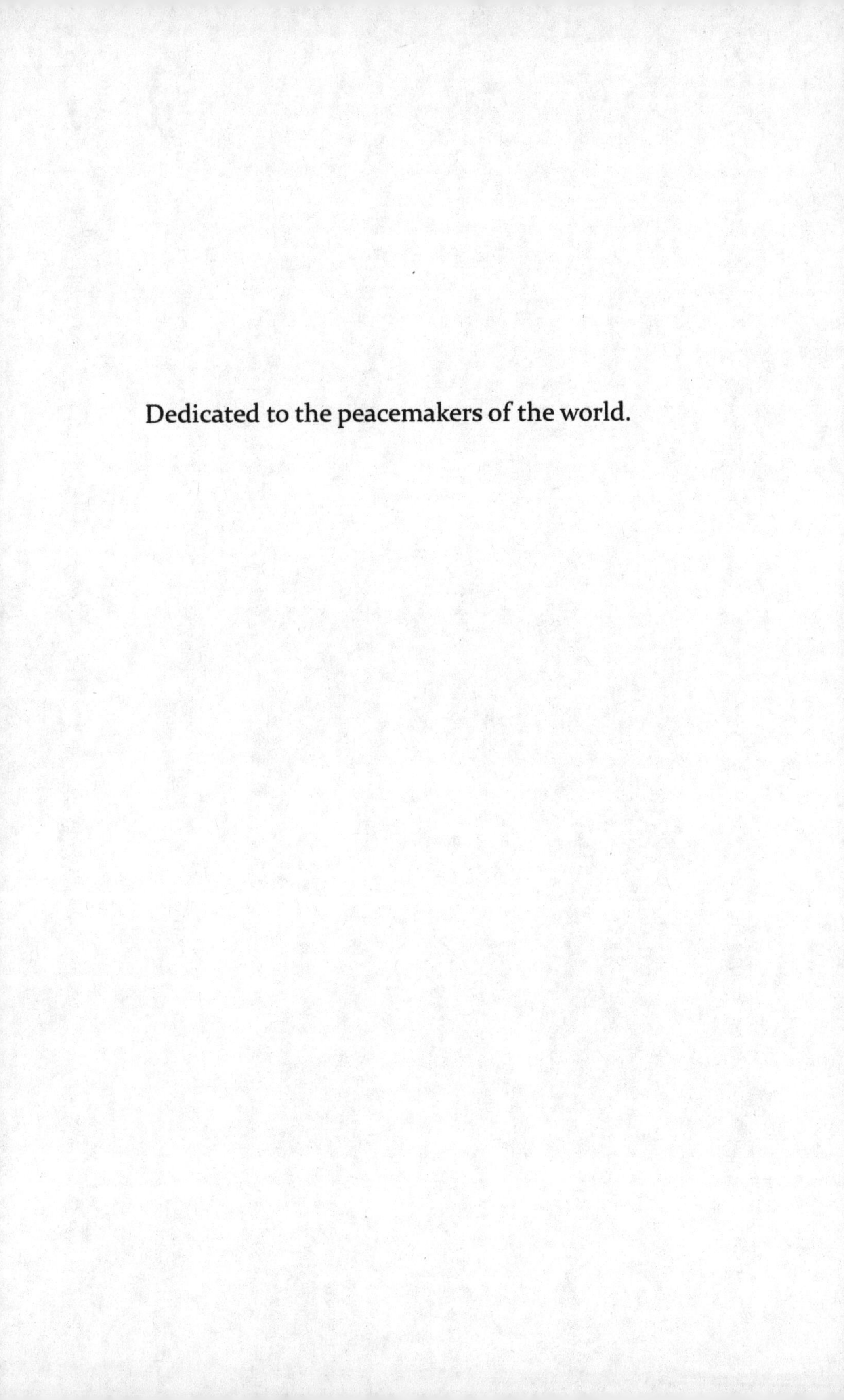

Dedicated to the peacemakers of the world.

Preface

Over the years I've witnessed many variations of the culture wars that have roiled the nation since the 1970s. Recently we've seen the rise of what's being called the 'cancel culture'—a movement to remove monuments or eliminate celebrations that some groups find offensive. Here in New Mexico we've had our share of these controversies, including the debate over whether to remove statues of Juan de Oñate and Kit Carson—or whether to eliminate the celebration of the Entrada. And we've seen the protest and destruction of the obelisk monument to Union soldiers on the Santa Fe Plaza.

In *Smokescreen*, the second in my Fernando Lopez Santa Fe Mystery Series, my detective finds himself caught up in the fractious debate over banning the Entrada, the Fiesta procession that re-enacts the Reconquest of Santa Fe by Don Diego de Vargas in 1692, twelve years after the Pueblo Revolt drove the Spanish out of Santa Fe.

The city, already on edge, plunges into chaos when a city councilmember who had negotiated a settlement in the Entrada dispute is assassinated. Both sides in the dispute blame the other for the murder. Detective Lopez must negotiate a middle path between those who support and those who oppose the Entrada while pursuing the assassin. The plot thickens when he discovers the murdered councilmember had been involved with a sex trafficking ring at Three-Hills Ranch south of the city.

In the end Detective Lopez must play the role of peacemaker, a role he's not accustomed to performing. It falls on him to bring the two sides together in a way that allows the city to move forward. In order to do that he must find the assassin and reveal the hidden truth about Three-Hills Ranch.

Part One: The Entrada

He heard the crowd roar in the park below as he walked down the arroyo toward the tree line. A three-quarter moon provided enough light for him to find his way through the white sand and boulders along the bottom. He passed what looked like a homeless camp above on the mesa, with a couple of them sitting in chairs out front of a tent waiting for the fireworks that accompanied the burning of the effigy they called Old Man Gloom. He crouched lower to keep out of sight.

When he neared the tree line, he paused to pull his black ski mask down over his face. He carried the rifle in its case and a Glock strapped to his belt. He crept up the arroyo bank slowly. As he reached the top he heard the distant sound of children playing. He paused, spotting the children about fifty yards away. They were roughhousing, wrestling and pushing each other down the embankment along Bishop's Lodge Road.

He froze, ducking down below the lip of the arroyo. He waited until the children ran into the trees chasing each other before moving out of the arroyo. He didn't think they had seen him. Moving faster now, he hurried into the protection of the trees. Tree branches scratched his bare arms as he squeezed through the thick underbrush searching for just the right spot. He found it next to a sturdy cottonwood. He looked around to make sure he was alone. Satisfied, he set up his tri-pod in the shadow of the cottonwood and then took his Barrett M82 out of its case and inserted the magazine.

From his position he looked down on a sea of people listening and dancing to the loud party music. While they danced, he surveyed the police presence around the park. He spotted a number of cops manning the gates and others inside the park policing the crowd. They would be trapped in place by the mass of late arrivers who clogged Bishop's Lodge Road in both directions as far as the eye could see. That would give him at least fifteen minutes to reach his vehicle on Rosario. More than enough time.

On the stage at the far end of the park stood city officials and Fiesta leaders. Dwarfing them, the fifty-foot puppet groaned and flailed its puppet arms in the air. When the music stopped, the crowd cheered madly in anticipation of the fire dancers. Quickly he placed the Barrett on its tri-pod. He adjusted the sight and the scope and then calculated the distance, making the necessary elevation adjustment using the turret. The shot looked to be just under one hundred yards, which would not be a problem for the Barrett. Especially since his target would be stationary and sitting down when Old Man Gloom went up in flames.

Using the scope now, he looked over the dignitaries assembled on stage until he found his target, a man whose photograph he'd studied carefully. He waited until the officials took their seats at the back of the stage and the lights in the park began to dim. Then he carefully focused the scope on his target, making the final adjustments to his front sight. He was ready.

Soon the dancers appeared on stage dressed in their fire-red costumes waving torches over their heads like batons. He watched the dancers approach the puppet and then pivot back. Backward and forward they danced, until they finally twirled and touched their torches to the paper maché puppet. The puppet burst into a ball of fire, with flames shooting up its torso and leaping out of its mouth.

As the crowd cheered wildly, desperate latecomers on the road poured across the field and into the trees to get a view of the park. Suddenly he found himself engulfed by an enormous crowd. Sensing danger, he quickly put away his rifle and tri-pod. Then he hurried back to the arroyo and headed for his car on Rosario.

His target didn't know how lucky he was. Tito Garcia would live another day.

1
Saturday

Detective Fernando Lopez of the Santa Fe Police Department sat at his desk brooding. He was still tired from last night's Fiesta celebration at Fort Marcy Park. He'd just finished the paperwork on a murder-suicide in Tesuque, a classic case of domestic violence. He found himself rehashing the entire episode and trying to figure out how it could have been prevented. Time and time again they'd warned the wife and encouraged her to leave her husband and seek help at the Esperanza Women's Shelter. They wanted her to get a restraining order and press charges, but each time she'd refused, even when the husband broke her arm and split her lip and blackened her eyes. Her drunken lout of a husband had used her as a punching bag.

Thinking about the sonofabitch infuriated him. They should have done something, thrown him in jail for a couple of days or given him to their intimidating colleague Antonio Blake for a little advice from an ex-Marine. At 6' 7" and 280 pounds, Antonio could be very persuasive to those who needed to be nudged back to the strait and narrow.

Now that he'd turned sixty, he found himself plagued by regrets and feelings of guilt in both his personal and professional lives. Lots of things he should have done differently–or better. These feelings seemed to come over him whenever he did paperwork, his least favorite part of the job. Paperwork required him to recount and in some cases justify their actions. He hated the constant retelling and rumination. He knew from years of experience that too much reflection would take him to the dark place he dreaded.

His nights were even worse. Ghosts of cases past haunted his nightmares. When things were bad he saw their angry faces nearly every night. Ghosts of the perpetrators he'd arrested and especially of the few he had no choice but to kill. Ghosts of the victims he'd failed to help, multitudes really. The sad, forlorn faces had come back to exact their revenge by haunting his dreams.

His wife said he was clinically depressed and advised him to seek counseling, but Estelle didn't understand what thirty years of police work could do to a person. No amount of counseling would change thirty years of bad memories.

He was saved from his brooding when Linda Stephens, the station dispatcher, buzzed him. He noticed a note of hysteria in her voice. "What's wrong?"

"Oh Jesus. Tito Garcia's been murdered."

"The City Councilman?"

"You got it."

"Holy shit!"

"A neighbor just called to report the body. Apparently Tito was on his way to work when someone shot him out front of his house on Upper Canyon Road. The Chief wants you to take over the investigation."

"Has Forensics been called?"

"Yes. You need the address?"

"No." He knew where Tito lived.

Tito had become something of a celebrity in Santa Fe because of his work on City Council and his private work as a professional mediator specializing in conflict resolution. Many Santa Feans believed Tito would be the next mayor.

Tito was known as the man who saved Fiesta by brokering a deal in the Entrada dispute. The much-loved, much-hated Entrada parade re-enacted the 1692 reoccupation of Santa Fe by Don Diego de Vargas twelve years after the Pueblo Indian Revolt of 1680 had driven out all the Spanish. Organized by the Caballeros de Vargas, the Entrada had become a symbol of cultural insensitivity to those Santa Feans who considered de Vargas a butcher because of his harsh treatment of the Pueblo People.

He remembered last year's Entrada riot only too well. He and the other cops stationed at the corner of Palace and Washington had no idea what was in store for them that day. They watched the parade come down Palace with the usual drummers and foot soldiers accompanying Don Diego de Vargas on his horse. He couldn't remember which of the caballeros had played the role of de Vargas.

"Murderers!" a woman suddenly shouted from the Plaza. She rushed into the street and threw a liquid-filled balloon at de Vargas. The balloon popped and doused the rider with red paint.

Behind the woman came an angry mob of protestors carrying signs and shouting insults. They physically blocked the street, disrupting the procession.

Other protestors on the Plaza began chanting "No more En-tra-da," and "No more gen-o-cide."

When protestors began smacking de Vargas and his horse with their signs, he and the other cops had to act. They wrestled signs out of the hands of troublemakers and pushed them back out of the street. He tackled and cuffed one long-haired young man who punched de Vargas' horse and then screamed, "Get off me you fucking pig!"

No one wanted a repeat of that fiasco, which resulted in multiple injuries, multiple arrests, and multiple incidents of vandalism in downtown Santa Fe.

Leaving his office, he walked down the long hallway to the front entrance. In the parking lot he found his cruiser and drove up Marcy to the Paseo and around to Canyon Road. He followed Canyon Road all the way up past El Farol, one of his favorite restaurants, to where it ended at national forest land. Tito's house abutted the national forest, snuggled against a stand of ponderosa pine with foothills climbing the side of the mountain behind the house. He parked outside the adobe fence next to the SFPD Forensics van. He saw Teresa and Miguel huddled over the body on the front porch of Tito's adobe house. Tito's red Toyota pickup was parked in the drive.

He climbed out of the cruiser and looked around, noticing a rickety guesthouse in back under the tall pines. The main house looked in better shape, even though the stucco around the front door had cracked in multiple places. The yard consisted of a riot of colorful hollyhocks—white, blue, red, and yellow. He noticed the fragrance of the alpine air as soon as he started walking toward the house, the scent of pine mixed with something else, sage perhaps.

He stopped briefly to check out the pickup. The driver's side door hung open, revealing a leather briefcase on the passenger seat. Nothing else caught his attention at first glance.

Tito's body lay face down on the concrete porch facing the front door. A set of keys dangled from the closed door, as though Tito was either locking or unlocking the door when he was shot from behind. He saw the entry wound in the middle of Tito's back and the huge pool of blood underneath the body.

"How long's he been dead?"

"No more than two hours," Miguel said, a bird-like little man with dark-rimmed glasses and a beak for a nose. "Looks like he was on his way to work. He took his briefcase out to the Toyota and then came back to lock the door. The bullet killed him instantly. Looks like a large caliber, may even a fifty."

Teresa sighed. "Now there'll be hell to pay in the city."

He didn't respond. He feared Teresa was right, that both sides in the Entrada dispute would blame the other side for Tito's murder.

While they worked on Tito, he looked around the yard. The shooter would have had an unobstructed view of Tito from the foothills that surrounded them. He noticed a trail that zig-zagged its way up the nearest foothill and decided to check it out. The trail started at the end of the street and rose quickly into the tree line. He took his time, climbing the trail slowly and looking for whatever the shooter might have left behind. He found nothing other than a dozen or so different footprints in the dust that would be of no help whatsoever. No spent cartridge, nothing.

On his way back he spotted an arroyo off to the East. Fifty or so yards down the ravine he saw what looked like a homeless camp, with tents, piles of garbage, and three people sitting around a dead campfire.

He hiked over to the camp, ignoring the smell of human feces as he approached. He recognized one of the three people in the camp. A nearly toothless old man named Bill who often panhandled on the Plaza. He didn't recognize the other two: an emaciated little man with long gray hair and beard, and a younger woman with long red hair. They didn't look any too happy to see him, probably thinking he'd come to close down the camp.

"How's it going, Bill?" He wanted to break the ice and show he was coming as a friend.

"Not so bad."

The wizened old man wore a stocking cap and an olive army jacket. He had two strands of party beads hanging around his neck, as though he'd just come from a New Orleans Mardi Gras celebration.

"Although I could use a little help, to tell you the truth. Can you spare a few dollars? How about a dollar for ever time you run me off the Plaza?"

He laughed. "I'll see what I can do, Bill. You help me, and I'll help you. How about that?"

Bill looked at him skeptically. "How can I help you?"

"By telling me if you saw anyone suspicious in the foothills over there this morning. Anyone hiding in the trees or carrying what looked like a rifle?"

"You mean, did I see who killed Tito Garcia."

"Exactly."

"Maybe I did, and maybe I didn't. Depends on how much we're talking about, my memory does."

He checked what bills he had in his wallet. "How about a ten spot? Does that refresh your memory?"

Bill smiled. "Yep, I think it's coming back to me. I seem to remember seeing one suspicious character on the trail this morning. A guy wearing khaki clothes, looked like one of them soldier types. He was carrying something...let me think...I jes' can't seem to bring it up. Maybe another tenner would help."

"I might have another five." He took the bill out of his wallet and held it up for all to see.

Bill reached up and snatched the bill. "Now it's coming back. Like I said, this soldier man was carrying something long in his hand, could have been a rifle case, I suppose."

"Yeah, and I saw a big fifty foot man with googly eyes and fire coming out of his eyes last night," said the emaciated man, interrupting Bill.

"Hah! That was Old Man Gloom, you dumb fuck!" The woman with red hair laughed and waved a bottle of wine at him.

"Who's Old Man Gloom?"

"The puppet they burned last night, don't you remember?"

The two of them traded insults until he opened his wallet again. Suddenly they fell silent, all eyes staring at him.

He handed Bill another five spot. "So did you see this guy in khaki shoot?"

"No, but I heard the shot. I was taking a piss over there when I heard the bang. Scared me half to death. I fell on my ass in the arroyo and bruised my hip. Mary there had to help me up."

"Dumb motherfucker!" the redhead said.

"Looks to me like you survived." He surveyed the camp. They had two Coleman tents set up and three Igloo coolers placed side by side between the tents. A bicycle leaned against a nearby tree.

"Any time you need information about what's going on around town, you know where to find me. I see everything."

"Okay, thanks. I'll keep that in mind."

He made his way back to Tito's house, dodging an overturned shopping cart abandoned in a patch of weeds. He didn't know what to make of Bill's story.

One thing he did know: no one in their right mind would consider Bill or his companions reliable witnesses.

2

He drove back downtown in his cruiser, thinking about Bill's description of a man in khaki who looked like a soldier. Could the shooter be someone in the military, or someone who had been in the military? A professionally trained sniper? He took the Paseo around to Marcy and drove down to the station on Washington Avenue. He parked in his usual space and walked into the station, where Linda greeted him at the front counter with some news.

"We put out a bulletin this morning asking if anyone saw a suspicious person on Upper Canyon Road last night," Linda said, laughing. "Even though pretty much everyone you see up there looks suspicious."

He loved Linda's sense of humor. An old hippie with long gray hair and a wicked sense of humor, she'd moved down to Santa Fe from Taos in the late 1970s after becoming disillusioned with living in the New Buffalo commune. He'd had a brief affair with Linda many years ago, his only indiscretion in the forty years he'd been married to Estelle. They'd broken it off to save their friendship...as well as his marriage.

"Good. You never know. I just spoke with a couple of people in a homeless camp up there."

Just then Antonio burst into the station out of breath. "There's big trouble on the Plaza. Ruben Ortega's raising hell. He's blaming the Pueblos and all those on the committee that banned the Entrada for Tito Garcia's murder. He wants to bring back the Entrada later this week."

Linda looked perplexed. "Why would the Pueblos want to kill Tito?"

Antonio waved off the question. "We need to act fast."

He frowned. Ruben had been one of the hotheads who'd argued for keeping the Entrada and to hell with the consequences. He'd been voted out of the Caballeros De Vargas leadership because of his militant politics. But he had his own followers, his posse as he called them. He'd been a troublemaker for years.

"Okay, let's go."

He followed Antonio outside and down the block to the Plaza. As they turned the corner onto Palace they saw the Plaza decked out in its Fiesta finest. Flags and banners waved from the Palace of the Governors, parts of which dated to the founding of Santa Fe in 1610. Food and alcohol booths lined the streets, with artisans selling their arts and crafts on the Plaza itself. Most of the crowd had moved down to the bandstand, where a Mariachi band played fast and loud.

Suddenly the music stopped.

Antonio pointed toward the bandstand. Ruben and his posse had just commandeered the stage, kicking off the puzzled musicians.

Ruben grabbed the microphone and started his rant.

"Friends, Tito Garcia was murdered this morning. Why? Because outsiders cancelled our Entrada. Because the Mayor and these outside groups and agitators banned our procession. What right do they have to come in here and tell us what to do? What right do they have to take away our history?"

The audience reacted with scattered applause and a few catcalls.

Ruben was undeterred. "Tell me, friends. Who's our mayor? That's right, Joe Martin. Is he native born? No. He's an outsider. He's an Anglo." Who's our Chief of Police? That's right, Larry Stuart. Is he native born? No. He's another Anglo. And so on and so on."

"So what?" someone from the audience yelled back.

Ruben stared down the crowd, daring anyone else to speak. He was a short, stocky man with a tanned, craggy face. A bulldog.

"I'll tell you so what: because he doesn't understand our traditions. Santa Fe has always been and will always be Hispanic. La Villa Real de la Santa Fe de San Francisco de Asis."

Now the audience started to get restless. They began arguing among themselves and with Ortega.

He began to fear an outbreak of violence.

"Friends, I'll tell you truly, Tito Garcia would still be alive today and none of this would have happened if the Fiesta Committee hadn't banned the Entrada!" Ruben shouted into the microphone. "This is the truth. Tito would still be alive. Long live the Entrada."

He motioned for Antonio to follow. They made their way to the bandstand. Ruben saw them approaching and quickly screamed into the microphone: "We re-enact the Entrada Tuesday at noon. Long live the Entrada." He pumped a fist into the air and held it there.

"Get off the stage, Ruben. If you want to be added to the list of performers, then contact the Bandstand Committee."

"Yeah, maybe I'll do that, Lopez. I never thought you'd be a traitor to your own people."

He grabbed the microphone and wrestled it from Ruben's hands, prompting his posse to move forward. Before they could, Antonio stepped in front of him and glowered at the five men in the posse. They held back.

"Fuck you, Lopez!" Ruben hissed, and stepped down off the stage. Before he disappeared into the crowd, he pumped his fist in the air again and shouted, "Entrada at noon Tuesday!"

The posse followed, eyeing Antonio carefully.

He turned to the Mariachi band, still waiting beside the stage. "Start playing, okay. Now!"

The musicians climbed back on stage and began playing again, easing tensions immediately. The crowd began to wander off toward to the food and alcohol booths lining the streets.

"That's quite a ploy," Antonio said, "blaming the groups who wanted to cancel the Entrada for killing the person responsible for cancelling it."

"He's a troublemaker, always has been."

They decided to remain on the Plaza for a while in case Ruben and his posse reappeared. Fortunately, the fiesta goers seemed more interested in cold beer and tacos than politics. As the afternoon wore on, the Mariachi band was replaced by flamenco dancers and then by Indian dancers from Tesuque Pueblo. Everyone seemed happy given the beer, the food, and the music.

At four he had to leave. "If Ruben returns, call me or Linda and ask for backup," he told Antonio and then walked down to Marcy Street, where he had an appointment with Tito Garcia's assistant, Tommy Baca.

He had spoken with Tommy on a couple of occasions but couldn't really claim to know him. Tommy was much younger than Tito and seemed to be something of a protégé. He helped Tito with multi-media presentations and sometimes filled in for Tito at meetings.

He found their office in the rear of a building on Marcy Street, not far from the *Santa Fe Independent*'s headquarters.

The sign on the door read: Tito Garcia, Mediation and Conflict Resolution.

The door was open, so he walked into the two-room office. He saw Tommy sitting at what had been Tito's desk, piled high with papers and reports and an old PC computer. The bookshelf along the rear wall sagged with books and heavily bound notebooks. Outside an open window he could see a courtyard, complete with a stone bench and a fountain that dripped water over a bronze statue. The sound of the falling water made him think the office would be a good place for mediation.

He walked into the office and extended his hand to Tommy. "Thanks for coming in to meet me."

"Oh, I've been sitting here all day." Tommy looked to be in his early thirties, a clean-cut young man wearing chinos and a blue polo. "I don't know what else to do with myself. I can't seem to focus on anything. I just can't believe Tito is gone."

"I think a lot of Santa Feans feel the same way."

Tommy leaned over the desk. "Tito was like a father to me. He treated me like a son...I guess because he didn't have a family of his own. His sister is taking care of the funeral arrangements. I'm just sitting here wishing I could do something to help...something."

He nodded, sympathetic. "He was good man. He helped a lot of people."

Tommy looked on the verge of tears.

"Will you continue his practice?"

"I don't know. He mentored me after I graduated from the University of New Mexico. He took me in as his assistant. I guess I'll keep the business going. I owe him that."

"Can you think of anyone who might want to harm him?"

"Hah! You're kidding, right? He received death threats all the time, especially over this Entrada thing. But even before that. In this business you resolve conflicts, but you also make a lot of enemies. Here, let me show you."

With that, he opened the bottom drawer of the desk and motioned for him to take a look.

"All of these letters are hate mail, some even include death threats. He kept all of them just in case something happened to him...so there would be a record, a paper trail to follow."

He looked at the stack of letters and notes jammed into the drawer. "Can I take a look at them?"

"Help yourself. Here, let me give you the most recent, most of them relating to the Entrada." He rifled through the papers and handed over a stack of about twenty-five letters.

He paged through the letters quickly. Most were letters from people angry about the cancellation of the Entrada. Others came from people dissatisfied with the results of Tito's mediation, or from people warning him not to take on certain cases or rule in favor of a certain faction. Many of them threatened Tito with physical harm.

"Could you give me all the letters going back a few months? I'll be sure to return them."

"Sure. Take what you want."

He took another stack of letters from the top, going back more than a year to before the Entrada controversy came to a head.

"Did Tito ever mention being physically attacked, or confronted, by any of these angry people? Did any of them show up here to threaten you?"

Tommy shook his head. "Tito never mentioned being attacked, but yes, some of the Entrada supporters have come by to express their dissatisfaction with us. Do you know Ruben Ortega?"

He laughed. "Oh yeah, we all know Ruben. He was on the Plaza earlier today raising hell. He's threatening to stage the Entrada Tuesday at noon come hell or high water."

"Well, he and his bodyguards came here and threatened us a couple of times, but they never physically attacked us...or hadn't until yesterday, if they were responsible for Tito's murder."

"Okay, but let us know if you receive any more threats. And watch your step. Since you were Tito's assistant, they may hold you partly responsible for the Entrada ban."

Tommy nodded.

"And I'll need to search Tito's house on upper Canyon Road when I get a chance. Do you have a key? Can you let me in?"

"No, I don't have a key, but Tito's sister is flying in from L.A. tonight to take care of his affairs. She'll be there tomorrow morning if you want to stop by. Her name is Delores Ruiz."

With that, he left Tommy sitting at Tito's desk and made his way back to the station. He decided not to go into his office, given the lateness of the hour. Instead, he climbed into his cruiser and headed home.

He dodged the Fiesta traffic on the Paseo and then turned left on Acequia Madre to the adobe he had shared with Estelle since their marriage forty years ago. The little adobe might be humble, but it was his retreat, his refuge from all the problems of the fallen world.

3
Sunday

Sunday morning Estelle went to church with their neighbor Maria. That left him alone with time to read through the stack of hate mail he'd brought back from Tito's office. Over the years Estelle had become more religious, working for the parish in a number of jobs, most of them non-paying. Currently she worked for the Saint Francis Immigrant Outreach Program. Santa Fe was a sanctuary city, which meant that hundreds of immigrants in the city needed everything from basic food, clothing, and shelter to legal services and medical care. Estelle and her co-workers in the program did their best to solicit and provide the needed resources.

He supported Estelle's dedication to the church and its work, as long as she respected his decision not to be involved. He believed in a material world, pure and simple. Occasionally he went to mass on Easter Sunday or Christmas Eve with Estelle and their two daughters but only to keep the peace and please Estelle. He figured it was the least he could do.

So when he heard the front door close, he took Tito's letters into his study and spread them out on his desk. As he examined them he made a list of the people who were angered by the cancellation of the Entrada. Some of the names he recognized, including Ruben's. His letter was short and to the point: "Tito, if you value your life, keep your hands off the Entrada."

Altogether there were about thirty letters that threatened Tito if he and his committee cancelled the procession. He decided to pass along the names to Manny, the newest detective on the force. Manny could check them out and report back ASAP.

Over half of the threatening letters concerned other issues. Some warned Tito not to take certain cases: a farmer's water rights, a rancher's mineral rights, a Boy Scout camp that had been shut down for code violations. Others concerned Tito's work on City Council and warned him not get involved in efforts to investigate complaints about a ranch south of the city or a proposed right-of-way for a land development adjoining San Ildefonso Pueblo.

Still other letters came from irate husbands angry about divorce settlements or greedy business partners dissatisfied with Tito's mediation. Pretty much anything that people could get angry about. Still, he reminded himself, it was possible one of these letter writers had gone through with the threat and murdered Tito.

He had finished with the letters by the time Estelle returned from church. "I wish you would surprise me one of these Sundays and come to church with me," she said, a trim, sprightly woman with steel gray hair who had aged much better than he had. He felt envious of her youthful looks and energy. There was no doubt in his mind that women aged better than men.

Noticing the time, he quickly placed the letters in a manila folder and took them with him to his cruiser. He first stopped back at Tito's house on Upper Canyon Road. He parked outside the adobe fence in front, again noticing the guesthouse in back under the tall pine trees. The front door of the guesthouse seemed to be ajar. He also saw a rental car parked in the driveway. Tito's sister had arrived, just as Tommy said.

He walked through the hollyhocks and up to Tito's porch. When he knocked on the door, it opened on Delores Ruiz staring at him. "I heard your car," she said, a small woman with dark hair and glasses, wearing slacks and a bulky turtleneck sweater.

"Detective Fernando Lopez from the Santa Fe Police Department."

"I've been expecting you. Mr. Baca mentioned you would be coming."

"I'm sorry about Tito."

"Thank you. Lots of people have sent their condolences. They're much appreciated."

He stepped through the door into the house.

"Yes, it was quite a shock when I got the message yesterday. We were never very close, because he was eight years younger. Still, he was my brother, my closest living relative."

"He was a good man. He helped a lot of people with their problems."

"I know. I'm very proud of him...what he chose to do with his life." She paused a moment and then added: "I can't say that about myself. I sell real estate in L.A."

"It's a profession," he offered.

"Well, let me show you around. I'm afraid Tito wasn't much of a housekeeper. He lived alone all his life, you know. Never married."

Walking into the living room he saw what she meant. Coffee cups, books, and papers littered every piece of furniture in the room. Clearly Tito had been a pack rat and someone who didn't bother to pick up after himself. The bedroom and kitchen looked much the same, with an unmade bed and dirty clothes on the floor in the bedroom and dirty dishes stacked on the table and the kitchen counters. He noticed a small room off to one side of the house, which turned out to be Tito's study.

"Would you mind if I looked through his study?"

"Help yourself. I'll be in the bedroom packing Tito's clothes. I guess I'll give them to Goodwill, unless you can think of a better idea."

"No, Goodwill sounds fine. Or one of the homeless shelters, they always need clothes."

He started with Tito's desk. He looked through the loose papers on top, mostly letters from lawyers and court documents relating to his work as a mediator. The file cabinet contained case files, which Fernando didn't have time to read. Next he examined several stacks of paper on the floor, beginning to feel overtaxed. Too much material to inspect--and he didn't even know what he was looking for.

He found Tito's brief bag in the closet, the kind that opened at the top with the initials T.G. imprinted on the brown leather. He brought the bag over to Tito's desk, took a seat, and pulled the handles apart.

What he found didn't seem all that interesting at first glance. The bag had two main partitions. The first contained a folder labeled "Entrada Committee." The folder included agendas and minutes from their meetings over the last few months. The second partition held papers relating to his work on the Santa Fe City Council. Fernando removed this material from the bag and went through it page by page. The papers referenced issues from crime to traffic, infrastructure to taxes. He looked but didn't find the agenda to the council's upcoming September meeting.

Last he examined the contents of the wastebasket. In addition to several empty beer cans and Chinese food containers, he found letters and envelopes, most from Santa Feans angry at the cancellation of this year's Entrada. One anonymous letter piqued his interest, however. It was a single sentence printed on an otherwise blank piece of paper: "Remember our agreement if you don't want to end up like the others." The paper wasn't folded. That told him it had been either hand delivered or slipped under Tito's door. He took the paper out to the hall table, where he would pick it up on his way out.

He couldn't stop thinking about the others. Who were the others? How had they ended up?

Just then he heard Delores call his name. "Detective Lopez...come take a look at this."

He walked back to the bedroom where she had been packing Tito's clothes in cardboard boxes.

"Look what I found," she said, pointing to a corner of the closet where several dresses and other items of women's clothing hung on hangers. "He must have had a lady friend, a girlfriend. Someone who spent the night."

The colorful dresses stood out among the drab surroundings.

A girlfriend?

He was thinking the same thing, having dismissed the possibility that Tito was a cross-dresser. Not the Tito he knew.

At any rate, these garments ran small and Tito, though not overweight, had been a hefty man.

"Looks like it. How well did you know Tito?"

"Not very, I'm sorry to say."

"Did he ever mention having a girlfriend or a live-in companion?"

He couldn't remember ever seeing Tito with a female companion, certainly not a woman who behaved like a girlfriend.

"No, but as I told you, we weren't close. And after I married and moved to L.A., we rarely spoke on the phone. I'm divorced now, but I've stayed in L.A. because my work is there."

He nodded.

"Not that I don't like L.A. I do. But I wish I'd made more of an effort to stay in touch with my younger brother, especially now that he's gone."

He quickly looked around the room. When he spotted the guesthouse outside the bedroom window, he asked, "By the way, have you gone into the guesthouse out back?"

"No, I haven't gotten that far."

"I think I'll have a look before I leave." He paused a moment. "Let me know if I can be of any help. And please let us know when you've made the funeral arrangements for Tito."

"Thank you."

On his way out he grabbed the letter he'd left on the table in the front hallway. He followed the sidewalk around the house to the guesthouse in back. It was built at the edge of the foothills, under the ponderosa pines that towered over its roof. As he approached the front door he thought he heard the sound of a door closing and then footsteps, as if someone were running away. Puzzled, he walked around the corner of the guesthouse and caught a glimpse of what he thought was a yellow piece of clothing as it disappeared into the thick forest on the mountainside.

He walked over to the ponderosa pines to take a look but saw nothing moving in the trees. He did see the hiking trail that began at the end of Canyon Road. He walked over to the hiking trail and followed it into the Santa Fe National Forest.

The trail eventually curved around to the left and then began a steep climb. The altitude bothered him more than he liked to admit. He stopped every few paces to get his breath before continuing. When he climbed out of the pines onto an outcropping of rock, he had a clear view of the city below. One branch of the trail broke off to the side and headed down toward East Alameda, the street that ran parallel to Canyon Road. At the top of East Alameda he caught another glimpse of the yellow clothing. So it hadn't been a mirage. He had seen someone exit the guesthouse and run into the forest. But who? The woman whose clothes they had found in Tito's bedroom? Or possibly an intruder?

He paused, debating whether to pursue the fleeing person or

return to Tito's house. Common sense told him he would never catch up with the runner. So instead of pursuing, he made his way back to the guesthouse. Finding the front door unlocked, he stepped inside and looked around the one-room structure. He found a Taos sofa bed with sheets and blankets, a kitchen table and chairs, and a sink and electric hot plate all squeezed into the one room. He also saw a corner bathroom with a sink and toilet and, hanging on the back of the door, a plastic clothing bag containing women's clothes, everything from underwear to slacks, dresses, and sweaters.

So Tito Garcia did have a female guest or companion living with him, he decided. Probably a younger woman, since the garments were a tiny size four and what he would describe as sporty.

Well, good for Tito. He was entitled to have a private life, including a young companion or live-in. What puzzled him was why she had run away. What was she afraid of?

4

A nearly deserted downtown greeted him as he drove back down Canyon Road to the Paseo. The Fiesta crowd had stayed home this Sunday morning, sleeping off yesterday's hangover before getting ready to repeat their excesses today. Fiesta lasted an entire week in Santa Fe and required stamina, not speed. He parked the cruiser in the parking lot on Washington Avenue and then walked into the station where he found Linda shaking her head, obviously pissed at something or someone. He hoped it wasn't him.

"Didn't know you were coming in today," he said.

"I didn't know either—until this morning."

"What happened to Doris?"

"Exactly the question I asked," Linda said. "Oh, by the way, we got a response on our hotline—asking if anyone saw a suspicious looking character on Upper Canyon Road."

He came over to the counter.

"Some kid—a thirteen-year-old named Ricky Lujan—said he was playing in the trees with some other kids when he saw two men dressed in uniforms hiding in the trees. He said one of them carried what looked like a guitar case. Here's his address," she said, handing him a piece of paper.

"Two men? Bill, the homeless guy I talked with yesterday, said he saw one man wearing khaki in the trees."

"Yeah, well, I don't know who's more reliable, a homeless bum or a thirteen-year-old," Linda cracked. "I'd say it was a toss-up."

He looked at the address again. "I'll check it out."

He decided to go see the kid now, before Fiesta traffic tied up the city streets. Back in his cruiser he drove up to Upper Canyon Road again and parked on the street in front of the address. When he knocked a small nervous woman opened the door. "Yes?'

"Detective Fernando Lopez," he said, showing her his badge. "Mrs. Lujan? I'd like to speak with Ricky."

"Why?"

"He called our hotline and reported seeing two suspicious men hiding in the trees Saturday morning when Tito Garcia was murdered."

She opened the door tentatively. "He doesn't know anything. I told him he shouldn't have called."

"Well, I'd like to hear what Ricky has to say." He brushed past her into the small but clean apartment.

She watched him walk into the living room and then followed. "Ricky. A police detective wants to talk to you."

Seconds later Ricky appeared in the living room, a pale heavy-set kid with a bad complexion. Ricky took a seat on the sofa and stared at him, expressionless. His mouth was closed tight.

He sat on a rocking chair across from the sofa. "Ricky, I'm Detective Fernando Lopez from the Santa Fe Police Department. You called our hotline and reported seeing a couple of suspicious characters hiding in the trees up in the foothills. Can you tell me anything more about the two men?"

He noticed Mrs. Lujan glaring at Ricky, as though warning him not to say anything.

Ricky stared straight ahead, not speaking.

"He doesn't know anything."

He ignored Mrs. Lujan. "Can you describe the object that one of the men was carrying? You said it looked like a guitar case. Could it have been a rifle case?"

The kid shook his head. Finally he spoke. "I didn't see anything."

"Why are you afraid to talk? Did someone threaten you, tell you not to talk to the police?"

"I didn't see anything."

They were wasting his time. He stood up, took out one of his cards, and handed it to the mother. "If you decide to talk, give me a call." Then he helped himself to the door, slamming it behind him.

Nothing pissed him off more than people who wasted his time. He had too much on his plate to put up with people who refused to cooperate. Whatever Ricky saw that night must have caused him to have second thoughts about sharing it. And the mother didn't help either.

He drove back to the station and complained about his experience with the Lujans to Linda.

"Don't blame me. I only report what comes across the hotline."

Not wanting to irritate her further, he walked down to the Plaza to help with Fiesta duty. The entertainment hadn't started, so he took the opportunity to grab a taco at one of the food booths and wash it down with a bottle of water. He watched the crowd closely for any sign of trouble, but Ruben and his posse were nowhere to be seen.

Later he made his way to the La Fonda Hotel for a change of scenery. Inside the carved wooden doors he encountered Ann Lewis, a member of the Santa Fe Fiesta Council, and Henry Ortiz, a spokesman for the All Pueblo Council of Governors. They huddled in the lobby conferring about something.

They flagged him down as he made his rounds through the hotel.

"Fernando, we hear Ruben Ortega is planning to hold the Entrada Tuesday at noon," Ann Lewis said, a tall woman with gray hair and glasses wearing a colorful fiesta dress. "Is that true?"

"That's what he says. I don't know how he can do it without the official backing of the Caballeros, the sponsoring group, but I wouldn't put anything past Ruben and his posse."

Ann Lewis looked at him gravely. "Just because Tito is dead doesn't mean our agreement is dead."

She said it accusingly, as though he had been conspiring with Ruben and other renegade Hispanics. "I agree."

"Well, we've scheduled a meeting of the Fiesta Council tomorrow morning at ten. Maybe you should be there. We need a plan of action."

"Yeah, because if the Caballeros march, I won't be able to control my people," Henry Ortiz added. "They're already riled up, you know. We thought we'd settled this Entrada thing once and for all with Tito and his committee. Now all these rumors we're hearing about Ruben. I don't know what will happen if he marches, but it won't be good. There could be violence."

"Okay, I'll come to the meeting. And if they do march without a permit, we can try to stop them."

Ann Lewis nodded. "Yes, but stopping them won't be easy...or peaceful."

"No it won't."

When he heard the music start outside on the Plaza, he made his way back to the bandstand. He listened to a loud salsa band enliven the crowd and get things rolling. Dancers of all ages gathered on the paved areas of the Plaza to dance. A country and western group followed the salsa band. He listened to a couple of cowboy tunes and then headed back to the station. He had a limited tolerance for cowboy lore.

He'd no more than sat down in his office and put his feet up on his desk, when Linda buzzed him.

"Fernando, there's a deputy sheriff from Santa Fe County here who wants to talk to a detective. Since you're the only detective here at the moment, you're appointed, my friend."

"Thanks. Send him back."

He heard Linda chuckle as she hung up the phone.

Seconds later a muscular woman with short-cropped dark hair in full uniform breezed into his office. She looked like a professional athlete, a soccer player or maybe a tennis player. She extended a hand over his desk. "Jodie Williams."

He shook her hand. "Fernando Lopez."

"I know who you are."

He was a bit put off by her brusque response but said nothing.

She took a seat across from him. "I need your help."

Something about her intrigued him. Her forwardness maybe. He felt a kind of tension between them. Not exactly sexual attraction, although that was part of the equation. At his age he didn't feel that way often. Then, again, he didn't encounter many women as impressive as Jodie.

"I just came from the morgue. We brought a body up from Highway forty-one near Galisteo. It was a young girl, maybe fourteen or fifteen. A hiker found her partially clothed and barefoot in a ravine alongside the highway. It looks like she was running from something because her feet were torn up from running on the rough terrain. It appears she died as the result of a vehicle hitting her from behind. Her spine was crushed and her skull was cracked open. And get this, there are tire tracks showing where the vehicle left the highway and actually swerved over to hit her. In other words, she was killed intentionally trying to run away from something."

"Or someone."

"Exactly.

"Who reported the body?'

"The hiker I mentioned earlier. He says he'd parked nearby and found her on the way back to his car. The coroner thinks she's been dead for about forty-eight hours. She looks Hispanic, but that's only my guess. We have no clue about her identity because she carried no ID... no purse, no papers, nothing that would identify her."

"A runaway? I mean from her family?"

"Maybe, but here's the thing," she said, her eyes fixed on his, holding him. "We found the body of another young woman along that same highway a couple of months ago. Again, no identification. Like the most recent, a motorist spotted this one partially clothed and barefoot on the side of the road. The medical examiners ruled the cause of death dehydration and hypothermia, but I'm deeply suspicious. I suspect she was raped and murdered. They found semen from at least three different men in her vagina. My guess is that she was beaten and gang-raped and then thrown in the ditch along the highway to die."

He shook his head. "I don't understand. Is there some sort of school or camp near Galisteo where these young women were staying?"

"Not to my knowledge, but the hiker who found this most recent body claims he saw several young women at a compound in what he called a box canyon just off the highway. Here, I made you a copy of his name and address."

She passed him the paper. It read: "Michael Roybal, 6521 Agua Fria Street N.E."

"I came to you because we're understaffed. We don't have the personnel to investigate these murders and you do."

Just like that. You do. She was giving him an order, not asking for help.

"And I want the people who did this brought to justice and locked up like the fucking animals they are, do you understand?"

"Of course."

She was so angry her hands were shaking on the edge of the desk. "These people are raping and murdering children...and they're going to pay for this."

She said it with such finality, such conviction, that all he could do was nod his head. "Okay. I'll go over to the morgue right after I'm done here. Can you show me where the body was found? Maybe tomorrow afternoon? In the meantime I'll try to track down Michael Roybal."

"Good. I appreciate your help," she said.

"Tell you what, I'll meet you at the junction of highways two eight-five and forty-one. Say three o'clock. There's a pull-off there where you can park."

With that, Jodie stood and walked out of the office quickly, as though she were in a hurry to get somewhere.

He watched her walk down the hallway and out of the station. He had second thoughts about taking on yet another responsibility. He had enough on his plate with Tito's murder and Ruben's threat to stage the Entrada Tuesday at noon. If Ruben made good on his threat there would be hell to pay in downtown Santa Fe. Still, he couldn't ignore two dead girls on a highway a few miles south of town.

Nor could he ignore Jodie.

On his way out he stopped briefly at the counter and said to Linda, "I'm on my way to the morgue."

She gave him a funny look and said, "Aren't we all."

5

He walked out to his cruiser in their parking lot on Washington Avenue and then drove to Christus St. Vincent Medical Center on St. Michael's Drive. He took the main elevator down to the basement where a cold tiled corridor off-limits to the public took him to the morgue. Miguel and Teresa greeted him in the front office, having just moved the body of the unidentified girl from their van to the dissection table for a forensic autopsy.

"Didn't expect to see you here," Miguel said.

He grunted. "Sheriff's short-handed. Asked me to help with the investigation."

"Well, take a look at our Jane Doe," Teresa said. "Must have been a real sadistic bastard to do this to a young girl."

She led him into the dimly-lit dissection room where red lights blinked on the wall panel and somewhere a machine whirred and beeped. Then he saw the girl.

"Oh fuck!" he said, turning away so as not to retch. He'd seen a lot of corpses here but none more disturbing than this one.

"Yeah…we haven't cleaned her up yet," Teresa said.

The white naked body lay bruised and swollen on the cold table. Dirt and dried blood caked her legs and feet as well as her face. Her upper body was twisted and bulging forward with her back and shoulders smashed in from behind. Multiple broken ribs punctured the skin of her chest. Her skull had cracked open in back from great trauma exposing the spongy brain matter. Her mouth was open wide in one final scream of horror.

Suddenly he felt dizzy. He closed his eyes and grabbed hold of the table. When he opened his eyes again he saw the lifeless face of his eldest daughter Flavia on the table. Then as he stared the sad, deformed face morphed into the face of Adela, his youngest daughter. He jumped back from the table.

Teresa reached over to steady him. "Are you okay?"

He did not respond. Was he okay?

"Take a look at this." Teresa pointed to the girl's breasts where bite marks were visible on both breasts.

"What? Was she attacked by wild animals?"

"Hah! Those are human teeth marks. Just look at the left nipple. It's almost bitten off."

He saw the purple marks under the dirt and grime.

"Have you determined the cause of death?"

"Well, we haven't examined the body yet, but from all appearances at the crime scene...and looking at the body...it looks like blunt trauma from being run over by a moving vehicle."

He nodded. "So you saw the tire tracks of the vehicle that hit her?"

"We did. It was clearly intentional. The car swerved off the highway and hit her from behind as she was running away."

"She would have died instantly," Miguel added.

"What about the other young woman whose body was found on that same stretch of highway last month? Do you remember? The sheriff I talked to said she didn't have any identification and wasn't wearing much clothing, like this one. Do you remember?"

"I do," Teresa said. "Except this one wasn't run over. We had a hard time determining cause of death, so we sent it to OMI in Albuquerque. They came back with dehydration and hypothermia as the cause of death."

"Did you buy that explanation?"

Both Teresa and Miguel looked skeptical.

"Not really," Teresa said, shrugging.

"Yeah, the hypothermia part was hard to believe," Miguel added. "September nights aren't that cold. But at the end of the day, the state medical investigator makes the call, so we didn't pursue the matter."

Teresa walked up to him. "Two dead naked girls on the same highway? Hard to believe it's a coincidence. What's going on down there, Fernando?"

He had no idea. He took another look at the dead girl and sighed.

"I don't know. I'm meeting the sheriff tomorrow afternoon. Maybe I'll know more then."

"I'll be in touch," he said and walked out of the dimly lit room into the long corridor to the elevator.

He found his cruiser in the parking lot and headed back downtown. He took Old Santa Fe Trail to the Paseo and turned right intending to go all the way to Marcy Street and then down to the station on Washington Avenue. But approaching the turnoff to Acequia Madre he said the hell with it and turned onto the street where he and Estelle had lived for the past forty years.

He had his fill of police work today. He'd be back at it early tomorrow morning, Right now he needed some well-deserved R & R.

6
MONDAY

He suffered through a sleepless night, tormented by nightmares of the girl he'd seen in the morgue. All night long he kept reliving the same scene: when he bends down to look at the distorted face on the metal table, the face transforms into the bruised faces of Flavia and then Adela. He awoke covered with sweat. The clock on the nightstand blinked five-thirty. Since he couldn't sleep, he decided to get an early start on the day. He managed to climb out of bed without disturbing Estelle, shower and dress and make himself a cup of coffee by six o'clock. He didn't bother to shave. At his age he didn't give a damn how he looked. On his way out of the house he grabbed a container of yogurt and a croissant to eat later in his office. Minutes later he was in his cruiser heading south on the Paseo to Agua Fria Street.

Michael Roybal's apartment turned out to be easy to locate. He found it in a run-down duplex with old tires and a rusted refrigerator thrown in what served as a front yard, a patch of dirt choked by weeds. He walked through the weeds around to the side door and banged on the flimsy screen door harder than he intended. For a moment he thought he'd knocked the door off its hinges. He banged again, this time not as hard. He didn't want to sound like the damned SWAT team.

Seconds later he heard a sound inside, like someone shuffling across the floor in slippers. When the door opened, he found himself looking at a young man with shoulder-length hair wearing briefs and a T-shirt who appeared to be half asleep.

"Yeah? What is it?" he asked, yawning and then rubbing his eyes with the back of his hand.

"Michael?"

"No, he's my roommate. I think he's asleep, you want me to get him?"

"Yes, please."

The young man turned away, stopped, and then turned back around. "By the way, who are you?"

"Detective Fernando Lopez, Santa Fe Police."

He showed the kid his badge.

The young man squinted into the bright sunshine. "What'd he do?"

He smiled. "Nothing. I just need some information that could help us with an investigation."

"Okay," he said, shuffling off to the rear of the house.

He heard the two men whispering, and then another young man wearing pajama bottoms and no shirt appeared in the doorway. He had pale skin and red hair and a closely cropped red beard. "I'm Michael Roybal," he said.

"Detective Fernando Lopez, Santa Fe police. Sorry to call on you so early."

Michael nodded.

"If you don't mind I'd like to ask you some questions about what you saw when you found the dead girl on Highway forty-one near Galisteo. It would help our investigation. Okay?"

"Sure, I guess."

"You told the sheriff you discovered the body on your way back to your car from hiking. Why didn't you see it on the way in?"

"Well, I started hiking right where I parked my car. It took me a while to find the trail. On the way back I followed the trail, which took me right past the body."

"Did you see anyone else around the area?"

"No, only a couple of cars driving by on the highway."

"You also said while hiking back in the hills you came across a compound of some sort. What did you mean by a compound?"

Michael paused a long moment. "You know, it was sort of like a camp. I mean there was a large house and what looked like a dormitory or bunkhouse...and then some other outbuildings."

He nodded. "You said you saw some young women there. What were they doing?"

"Yeah, I saw five or six girls walking around the grounds."

"Could you tell how old they were?"

"They looked like teenagers from where I was standing. I didn't get very close. The place was surrounded by three hills, and there was an armed guard out front by what looked like a guardhouse. Didn't look like a very friendly place. And it was kind of weird."

"What do you mean weird?"

"Well, for one thing there was a helicopter pad—and a helicopter—behind the house. And I didn't see a road leading into the compound. I saw vehicles, but no driveway. I don't know how you would get there by car."

He didn't like the sound of this. Clearly the people in charge didn't want visitors. "So how did you find the place if there wasn't a road?"

"It's easy, really. There's an old cattle or animal trail about a hundred feet south of where I found the girl. It takes you across the mesa and up on top of the nearest hill, about a mile or so. From there you can see the compound down in the valley between the three hills."

He stood back from the door, considering. "Did anyone see you up there on the hill?"

"Not that I know of. I kept low. To tell you the truth, the place scared me. Bad vibes. I turned around and came right back to my car. That's when I saw the girl in the ravine all bloody and covered with mud. Freaked me out even more. I mean, I'd never seen a dead person before. I called the sheriff and waited until they arrived. Took forever."

"Okay. Here's my card. Call me if you remember anything else."

Michael watched him walk away from the doorway and then went back inside the apartment.

He dodged the weeds and the old tires as he walked back to his cruiser. He followed Agua Fria back to the center of town to Washington Avenue and parked in the station lot. First he went next door to the Great Burrito Company and bought a large coffee to go and then walked back to the station.

Benny, the night dispatcher, was still on duty at the front counter. "I have one message for you, Fernando."

Benny handed him the slip of paper. It was from Miguel in Forensics: "Fernando, ballistics results are in for Tito Garcia shooting.

Bullet was fifty BMG. Possibly from a Barrett M eight-two or M ninety-five. Be careful."

Great, he said to himself, so we have a rogue professional sniper loose in Santa Fe. Wait until the chief hears this. Chief Stuart tended to be volatile anyway. This would send him over the edge.

It turned out the chief already knew, as he discovered as soon as he walked into his office and found the man sitting at his desk. The chief wore his usual suit and tie, with his granny glasses and thinning gray hair making him look older than his forty-some years. He threw out his arms, as if asking for something, help maybe.

"Jesus Christ, Fernando, did you read the ballistics report? We have a killer stalking Santa Fe with a nine or ten thousand dollar sniper rifle who can kill anyone, anywhere, at any time. What the fuck are we doing about this?"

By 'we' he knew Stuart meant him.

"Tell me, what the fuck are you doing? It's your investigation."

He took a seat on the other side of the desk and listened to Stuart shout, trying to stay calm. One of them had to stay calm. It wouldn't be the chief.

The bad blood between him and the chief never seemed to end. As a consequence he had a reputation for being prickly. But who wouldn't be prickly after watching one Anglo after another being promoted ahead of him. It took him twenty years to make detective. Compare that to the three years it took the chief's nephew to make detective. What a joke. Dickless Andy as the other cops called him had the lightest workload of any of them.

Even worse, he got it from both sides. To the Anglos, he was a Chicano with an attitude. To the La Raza agitators and hotheads, he'd sold out his own people to work for the Man. He'd set himself against the People.

Well, fuck all of them. He just wanted to do his fucking job without being harassed. Call him old fashioned, he happened to believe that murderers and other scumbags should be off the streets.

"So do you have any leads on the shooter?"

Suck it up, he told himself.

"No," he said, shaking his head. "I suppose we should suspect one of the Caballeros angry that Tito and his committee cancelled the Entrada. That would seem logical."

"Yes, because why would anyone from the Pueblo Council murder Tito when Tito gave them what they wanted? It has to be one of the Caballeros. What about this Ruben Ortega fellow? He's been causing trouble, right?"

"Maybe. He's threatening to stage the Entrada tomorrow at noon with or without official support. But I don't know. I've known Ruben for a long time. I just don't know that he or any of his friends have the professional skills to pull off something like this, if you can follow me."

The chief looked at him skeptically, rocking back and forth in his chair. "Okay, let's do this. Let's run a check and see who among the Caballeros served in the military and may have training as a professional sniper. There can't be many candidates, not in Santa Fe anyway."

He volunteered Manny, their youngest detective and wizard of online data base research.

When the chief left, he breathed a sigh of relief and retrieved the folder containing Tito's hate mail. He wanted to check one letter sent by the owner of a ranch complaining of the goings-on at an adjoining property. The owner, A. J. Hoke, wanted Tito to ask City Council to investigate this property, which was owned by a Robert Warner Esq. Hoke's address was listed as Galisteo, not far from where the two dead girls were found along Highway 41.

He had to laugh out loud. You didn't find many 'Esquires' in Santa Fe, although that could be changing with the arrival of more and more wealthy people from the East and West Coasts. Did wealthy Anglos still refer to themselves as 'Esquire,' he wondered. He couldn't imagine any Hispanic or native Santa Fean ever using that term.

Anyway, Hoke's letter to Tito begged the question: what were the complaints about this property that Tito was taking to City Council? He figured only Tito and possibly his assistant would know.

With that in mind he dialed Tito's office, hoping to reach Tommy. No one answered, so he left a message asking Tommy if he had any specific information about the nature of Hoke's complaints about Robert Warner. He left both his office and cell phone number on the message and asked Tommy to call him back as soon as possible.

He checked the time. He still had over an hour before the Fiesta Council meeting at City Hall. He finally had time to eat his breakfast, the yogurt and croissant he brought from home.

When he finished, he made a list of the men who ran with Ruben, his so-called posse. Larry Aragon, Jim Gurule, Benny Montoya, Sam Naranjo, and one big guy with a graying goatee who usually wore a Cabela's baseball cap who he didn't know. If he remembered correctly, Aragon had served in the first Iraq War either in the Army or Marines. He didn't think Gurule, Montaya, or Naranjo had military service. He had no idea about the big guy's background.

He waited until nearly ten o'clock. to walk over to City Hall, too long as it turned out because as soon as he opened the door he saw the hallway jammed with people jockeying for position. Both supporters and opponents of the Entrada carried signs and waved them overhead. At one point an activist carrying a UNITED, NOT DIVIDED sign locked sticks and fenced with an activist wielding a HANDS OFF OUR TRADITIONS sign. Like a damned sword fight.

He tried to push through the crowd but could only get within a hundred feet of the room where the meeting was being held. He looked for but didn't see Ruben or any of his posse out in the hallway.

The noise was deafening. He had no idea if the meeting had started because everyone in the room seemed to be shouting and arguing at once. None of the committee members could get a word in over the shouting.

Finally he heard a gavel slam down and a woman who sounded like Ann Lewis shout, "Meeting cancelled!"

The shouting continued for a few minutes but gradually died down as people began to leave the room, jostling for space in the crowded hallway. He waited for the room to empty, wanting to make sure everyone got out safely. The last person to leave was Ann, who stuck her head out of the door and looked around, as if checking for assassins.

"Fernando. Can you walk me to my car?" The tall wisp of a woman stepped out of the room and took his hand.

"Absolutely."

"Let's go out the back way," she said. "I'm really frightened. Civil discourse has broken down. Civility itself has broken down. If the Caballeros go ahead with the Entrada tomorrow afternoon, we're going to have a full-scale riot on our hands. And then what?"

"Well, we hope not. We'll be out in force on the Plaza. If there's violence, we'll do our best to control it."

She wasn't reassured. "Tito worked so hard to prevent this. We wanted to schedule a memorial in his honor, maybe something at Saint Francis Auditorium. I just can't believe it has come to this."

"Passions run high."

"I know I'm Anglo and this is not my culture, but it seems so juvenile to me. I mean, riding a horse down Palace Avenue wearing armor and a sword. Like little boys playing soldier."

"Don't say that out loud. It might take more than one cop to get you out of here alive."

She glanced at him and then up and down the hallway.

7

After lunch he decided he needed to pay Ruben a long overdue visit. He and Ruben had known each other since they were students at Santa Fe High. Up until about ten years ago they had been friends. Then came the Tex-Mex incident. Ruben was having a beer at the La Fonda bar when a Texan tourist came swaggering into the bar and got hot under the collar because the bartender was talking to Ruben and not serving him. The Texan made the mistake of referring to Ruben as a 'Mexican' and all hell broke loose. The two men busted up the bar pretty bad and in the end Ruben was arrested because he'd done more damage to the loud-mouthed Texan than the Texan had done to him. In short, Ruben had never forgiven him because he happened to be the arresting officer.

Because of their history, he asked Antonio to go along as backup.

"About time...I'm surprised you waited so long to interrogate that disagreeable sonofabitch," Antonio said, not a big fan of Ruben's.

"That's exactly why I waited so long,...because he's a disagreeable sonofabitch."

So they took his cruiser out on the Old Las Vegas Highway to Apache Canyon. Ruben had a 20-acre spread in the canyon, where he'd built his adobe home and a frame workshop for his business as a contractor/handyman. To get to Ruben's property you had to drive across a small stream that usually ran dry in the summer months. During the spring run-off you had to park on the other side of the stream and walk across a shaky wooden pedestrian bridge held up by cables attached to trees on either side of the stream.

Today the stream was dry, so he revved up his cruiser and bounced over the rocky bottom of the stream to the other side. They drove past the house to the workshop, where Rubin's Jeep and two other cars were parked. He pulled in behind the Jeep and turned to Antonio. "Don't start anything, okay? Let's keep this civil."

"I don't start things, I finish them."

"I know, but just don't touch anyone, okay?" he asked, fully aware of Antonio's past and the damage he could do if someone crossed him.

He led the way to the open doors of the workshop, which resembled a mid-size barn. Inside it contained a range of machines and construction equipment, everything from a back-hoe to a row of table saws, lathes, and power tools. Ruben and two of his posse, Larry Aragon and Benny Montoya, stared at them as they entered the workshop and made their way to the rear of the shop, where Ruben and the others stood at a metal work table.

On the table they had laid out the ceremonial accoutrements they would wear in staging the Entrada—helmets, swords, leather belts, and period clothing.

"Well, well, I wondered when you would show up, Lopez. And I see you brought your gorilla along with you."

"I thought I smelled something," Benny added.

Antonio took a step toward Benny but then stopped himself.

He opened his arms wide. "It's my job, Ruben. I keep telling you this."

"So I remember."

"Here's the thing. I need to ask you some questions. I can bring you in for questioning, or I can do it here. It's up to you. I'm doing you a favor by coming out here."

Ruben stared at him and then laughed. "That would be a first—you doing me a favor."

"You almost killed that Texan, Ruben. What did you expect us to do, arrest him? He was in the hospital for a fucking week."

"So what? He deserved what he got. Do you like to be called a fucking Mexican?"

"No, but can we just move beyond the damned Tex-Mex incident?"

Ruben remained silent.

"Now...you sent Tito a threatening letter saying if he valued his life he should keep his hands off the Entrada. Well, Tito didn't keep his hands off the Entrada, and now he's dead. You see the problem?"

"Lots of people sent Tito hate mail," Ruben snapped. "He betrayed us. He sold out to the fucking Anglos. That's our heritage, Fernando, in case you've forgotten. You can't just take it away from us because a bunch of liberal, politically correct assholes feel threatened by it. It's none of their goddamn business. They should keep their noses out of our history."

"Wait a minute, Ruben. We don't do a lot of things we used to do... out of respect for other cultures and to keep the peace."

"Fuck the peace. I'd rather have the Entrada."

"And that's exactly why I'm here. Where were you the morning Tito was killed? Home?"

"Of course I was here. You can ask my wife, she's in the house right now if you want stop by and check my story."

"I might do that."

Then he turned to Larry and Benny. "Do either of you own a fifty caliber rifle? Larry, you were in the first Iraq war, as I recall. Did you ever use a fifty caliber?"

"Yeah, so what?"

"Do you still own a fifty caliber rifle?"

Larry laughed, a tall thin man with a narrow face and a tight seventies moustache. "Do you have any idea how much a sniper rifle costs, ese? They're too rich for my blood."

"Do you know anyone else who has one?"

"Why are you asking?"

"Because Tito was killed by a fifty caliber bullet."

Larry shook his head. "Jesus..."

"Look, I'm sorry about Tito," Ruben said. "I liked Tito. He was a friend until all this started. But tradition is tradition. It's our lifeblood, Fernando. We can't just give it up every time someone complains. Goddamn it, you're from the same blood I am. You of all people should understand."

"I do, but we have to find a way to get along, Ruben. If you march tomorrow, you'll rip the community apart."

"Hah! That happened a long time ago, when the fat cats from L.A. and New York started moving to Santa Fe."

"Okay, look, I'm asking you personally not to stage the Entrada tomorrow. As a favor to me. We used to be friends. Remember?"

Ruben laughed. "Yeah, before you busted my ass."

He continued. "Let's find another way to celebrate our presence in Santa Fe. You understand? Our presence, not our conquest. It's a multicultural city, that's what we should be celebrating."

Ruben did not respond. He stood with his arms crossed, staring at him.

There was nothing more to say.

On the way out Antonio asked, "Do you want to stop by the house and ask Ortega's wife if she'll vouch for him?"

"No, she would only repeat what he said."

"So what do you think?"

"About Ruben? No. It's not that simple."

8

He hated being late, but today he couldn't help it. After dropping off Antonio, he left immediately for his three o'clock appointment with Jodie. He pushed his cruiser past the speed limit driving southeast out of Santa Fe on I-25 and then turning directly south on Highway 285. Once he left the interstate the landscape changed from national forest to desert mesa dotted with rock formations and distant buttes. Sage and chamisa grew wild on both sides of the deserted highway.

Approaching the turn-off to Highway 41 he saw Jodie's cruiser parked on a gravel lot beside the highway where a lone picnic table and an overflowing trash can offered a less than ideal stopping point for weary travelers or picnickers.

He parked behind Jodie and walked around to the front of her cruiser. She didn't move. She sat behind her steering wheel in full uniform wearing dark blue sunglasses.

"Follow me." Yet another command. She continued to impress him with her take-charge attitude.

She drove off down Highway 41 without waiting for him.

He hurried back to his cruiser and followed, trying to keep up with her. She drove much faster than he did, but he had no trouble keeping track of her in the open terrain. When she pulled off on a grassy shoulder, he did the same. She had already climbed out of her cruiser by the time he'd parked his.

"What took you so long?"

"Uh...the speed limit."

"Let me show you where the girl died," she said, ignoring him.

He followed her down the road to an embankment alongside a ravine. She climbed down into the ravine and pointed to a depression. "This is where we found the body, partially covered with brush and leaves and a thin layer of dirt. Whoever did this must have tried to cover her up with whatever was available in the ravine."

He looked around the bottom of the ravine and then climbed back up the embankment.

"Yeah, that's where the car hit her from behind, but take a look at this."

She joined him on the embankment and pointed to tire tracks that had swerved off the road onto the embankment. "You can see where the vehicle came off the highway and hit her intentionally and then swerved back down to the highway. There's traces of skid marks on the pavement where they stopped after hitting her so they could come back and hide the body."

He looked to the south. "So she was running north trying to get away from something down there."

"Exactly. You can see her bare footprints in the sand coming up here from the mesa."

"Let's take a look."

She led him down to a sandy patch at the foot of the embankment. "Here, see her footprints as she came up to the embankment? She was running. Running fast."

They followed the footprints across the ravine to a barbed wire fence, where two strands of the barbed wire had been pulled far apart allowing for entry. They stepped through the opening and into what looked like grazing land. Ahead they saw an animal trail, a thin ribbon of dirt, leading to a series of three hills on the western horizon. On the sandy trail they found intermittent footsteps indicating the girl had run down the trail, coming from the direction of the hills.

He stopped. "So this is the trail Roybal took to the top of the first hill, where he claimed to see a some kind of compound or ranch."

She glanced at her watch. "Do you have time to check it out?"

"No, but let's do it anyway."

They started up the trail, which climbed gradually up a long slope. When they came to a sheet of rock the footprints disappeared. They looked on the other side of the rock bed but found nothing.

"She must have come around the hill, not down, and joined the trail here," he said. "We can try to pick up her trail, or we can go to the top of the hill. What do you want to do?"

"Let's go to the top of the hill. I'd like to see what this mysterious compound looks like."

So they made their way up the long slope toward an outcropping of red rock that jutted vertically into the sky like some sort of monument. He figured the rock must be at least a half-mile away, maybe more. He struggled to keep up with Jodie, who marched ahead full speed without once looking back. Once again he wondered if she had been an athlete.

When they reached the top he couldn't resist asking her the question he'd been pondering. "Are you a former athlete or something?"

She gave him a stern look. "I was on the women's basketball team at UNM. I stay in shape. Don't you?"

Again he felt the static between them. He liked her. She seemed as prickly as he was.

From the outcropping of rock at the summit they looked down on a valley surrounded by three hills, just as Roybal had described it. The ranch included a sprawling house, what most people would call a mansion, with four wings and a courtyard in the center. On the opposite side of the valley stood a barracks of some sort, with a barn and a three-car garage off to the side. A guardhouse blocked the entrance to the valley.

Roybal hadn't seen a road leading into the compound, but he saw a narrow gravel road leading out past the guardhouse.

Jodie pointed to a bench on the long porch of the barracks where two young women were sitting together holding hands. "Look... teenagers, just like the two who were murdered on the road."

He noticed the helicopter on the helipad behind the house. "What do you think this place is?"

"I don't know, but I don't like the looks of it. Why all the secrecy?"

From where they stood, leaning against the outcropping of rock, they were in full view of the valley below. While they talked, a man stepped out of the guardhouse talking on a walkie talkie.

Seconds later an All Terrain Vehicle appeared, shooting out of the nearest out building and revving its engine. They watched it roar up the winding trail toward them and eventually come to a stop in a cloud of dust.

The man who stepped off the ATV was a big muscleman wearing a khaki uniform and cap. "Can I help you?" he asked in a gruff voice.

"Yes, you can," Jodie shot back, showing her badge. "We're here investigating the murders of two young women."

The big man seemed taken aback. He hesitated before speaking. "Murder? Where?"

"Their bodies were found on Highway forty-one not far from here. One was intentionally run over by a car, and the other was raped and strangled. Neither of them had IDs. Do you have any idea who they might be?"

"No, all this is news to me."

"By the way, what is this place?" he asked.

"This is private property."

"Well, why don't you tell us what's going on here, or we'll come back with a search warrant."

The man considered for a moment.

"We're a private facility. We treat wealthy young women with drug or alcohol problems. Most of our clients come from the Dallas / Ft. Worth and Houston areas. They come here to detoxify. We keep our work very private—at the request of the families."

"And who are you?"

"I'm the head of security. They call me the Foreman."

"The Foreman," he repeated. "And you have counselors and psychologists down there who will verify all this?"

"Yes, but our charge is to keep our work private, off the beaten path. Secret, if you will-"

Jodie stepped forward, interrupting him. "So the young women who were murdered, were they your clients?"

"No, none of our clients are missing."

"What's the name of your facility?"

"Three-Hills Treatment Center. We call it Three-Hills Ranch for short."

"How many patients do you have at the moment?"

"Right now? Six."

"And what's Robert Warner's role in all this? Is he one of the counselors or psychologists?"

The Foreman moved away, eager to be off. "He's the CEO. He's in charge of the operation."

When they did not immediately respond, the Foreman continued, "So I hope you understand our need for privacy. Both our clients and their families expect it. And pay for it."

With that, the Foreman climbed back on his ATV and revved the engine. Then he shot off down the winding trail to the ranch, leaving them in a cloud of toxic fumes.

The fumes made him cough. "I think we better get a search warrant."

"Yes. He's lying through his teeth. Let's get out of here."

He followed her back down the trail.

9
TUESDAY

Tuesday morning he drove to the station early. He skipped his usual cup of coffee at the Great Burrito Company and went into the station. He frowned when he saw John Hammond of the Coalition to End the Entrada waiting for him in the lobby. Not the way he wanted to start the day. He knew exactly what Hammond intended to say because he'd heard it a hundred times from Hammond and other members of his group. They never let up.

He preempted the conversation, buying time. "Give me a few minutes to take care of some things, John."

He walked on down the hallway to his office.

Everyone in Santa Fe remained on edge, worried about what would happen if Ruben followed through with his threat to stage the Entrada at noon. Better to keep busy so he wouldn't dwell on the impending trouble. He first met with Manny, who had contacted all those who had written threatening letters to Tito. All of them had alibis for where they were Saturday morning when Tito was murdered. All of them denied owning or ever using a .50 caliber rifle. In other words, they had absolutely no leads as to who murdered Tito.

"Sorry," Manny said.

"Not your fault."

"What else can I do to help?"

He thought for a moment. "Well, you might stop by Ricky Lujan's apartment and ask him again about the men he saw in the trees on Upper Canyon Road. Maybe his memory will return if we keep paying him visits. It would help if he could give us even a rough description of the two men he saw in the trees that night, something more than they were dressed in uniforms. And ask him if he's sure he saw two men. Another witness claims to have seen only one."

"Will do. I'll pay him a visit after school. Maybe his mother will be at work and he'll be more willing to talk."

"Good idea."

He watched Manny walk out of his office.

He waited a few more minutes before calling in Hammond. With a bit of luck, Hammond may have grown tired of waiting and taken off. He could always hope so anyway. Sadly, he found Hammond still sitting in the lobby, tapping his foot on the ugly green floor tile.

"Are you trying to avoid me?" Hammond asked, an aging community activist who had been giving police and other city officials a hard time since the seventies. Hammond had risen to prominence as a hell-raiser during the La Raza and Vietnam protests. Like Linda, he'd moved down to Santa Fe from Taos after getting tired of the Dennis Hopper drug scene in Taos.

"Why would I want to avoid you, John?"

He noticed the old hippie's appearance never seemed to change: long gray beard and ponytail, blue jeans, and a T-shirt that read "Fight the Power". Except for a few wrinkles and the gray hair, Hammond looked pretty much the same as he did forty years ago back in the fighting seventies.

Hammond followed him back to his office and helped himself to a seat, where he sat with folded arms staring straight ahead. Seconds passed, and still Hammond kept staring without speaking. He seemed to be meditating or maybe just spaced out. That wouldn't be the first time.

"So...John, what can I do for you?" He figured the sooner he heard the man's complaint, the sooner the guy would leave.

"You know why I'm here, Fernando. On behalf of the Coalition to End the Entrada, we want you to stop the parade today. I mean, come on, man, we had an agreement to eliminate the Entrada from Fiesta, and now they want to renege on the agreement. Well, they can't do that, man, they already agreed. It's too late."

"Okay."

"Wait, are you patronizing me? Is that what you're doing?"

He shrugged.

"You've always been a stand up guy, but now you're pissing me off. You and the other cops aren't doing a damn thing about this situation."

"Not true."

"I mean, you're the only cop who'll even talk to me anymore. The others just walk away."

"John, listen to me, we'll do the best we can. You just have to understand the Entrada runs deep in Hispanic culture. It's our history, our tradition. We don't let go of it easily."

"So is racism in the South, man. The southern states are taking down their Civil War statues and all that Confederate shit. We need to do the same thing here with our conquest monuments and celebrations. I mean, who celebrates colonialism today? Nobody. Come on, Fernando. The people have spoken."

That word again, the people. Everyone claimed to represent the people. Every side of every issue had its own definition of the people.

"Like I said, we intend to keep the peace."

Hammond stroked his beard, nodding. "Because if the cops don't stop the Entrada, then we'll have to stop it, and that'll get ugly, man."

"That would be a mistake. You and the other groups opposing the parade need to let us take care of the peace. We don't want anyone to get hurt, that's the long and short of it, okay?"

"Yeah, that's what I'm saying. We don't want anyone to get hurt."

He stuck his hand over the desk. "Then we're in agreement. Thanks for stopping by."

Hammond looked at his hand for a few seconds and then reached across and shook it weakly. "Okay, man, I guess we settled that."

"Yes, we did."

Hammond flashed him the peace sign as he departed, meandering down the long hallway to the door.

After the old hippie wandered off he sat at his desk considering his next move. They seemed to be at a dead end with Tito's murder, waiting for something to turn up. He knew cases like this could run hot and cold. He wasn't particularly worried, as long as the chief didn't start berating him again, blaming him for the lack of progress in the investigation. All the cops knew the chief wasn't a patient man. When the business community started barking, the chief started looking for someone to blame, usually him or one of the other Chicanos.

With time on his hands, he decided to walk over to the Great Burrito Company. A late cup of coffee was better than no cup of coffee. So he walked down the hallway and asked Linda if she wanted anything.

"Yeah—a pay raise," she cracked.

"Can't help you there."

He stepped outside and walked down Washington to the Great Burrito Company. Once he had his coffee he put a lid on the paper container and started to walk back to the station.

He hadn't gone more than fifty feet when his cell phone rang.

"Fernando, it's Tommy Baca." The voice was distant and kept breaking up. "I'm sorry I haven't been in touch...but I wanted to let you know that I have to leave town for a while. We're in danger."

He took a seat on a nearby bench. "We? Who's this we?"

As far as he knew, Tommy was single. He had never mentioned being married.

"I'll explain everything as soon as I can. I think we're being followed. We have to get out of town fast, before they find out where we're hiding. I'm afraid of these people."

"You mean the people who killed Tito?"

"Maybe, I'm not sure. All I know is I received a death threat and now I'm being followed. We have to get away."

"Tommy, please listen to me," he said. "Don't run. Stay here and I can protect you. I can give you a police escort. I can assign officers to stay with you at all times. I can keep you safe here, but if you run there's nothing I can do for you. You'll be on your own."

"I appreciate your offer, but you don't understand. These people are trying to kill us. We have to get away."

"We who?" he asked again, but the only response was a click ending the call.

10

High noon arrived unseasonably hot in Santa Fe, with everyone on edge. Both supporters and opponents of the Entrada packed the Plaza. Caballeros members and sympathizers lined Palace Avenue in order to protect the procession when it came down Palace. The protestors had gathered in the center of the Plaza, waiting for the bugle call. They carried homemade signs with catchy slogans like UNITED, NOT DIVIDED and END THE ENTRADA. One group had hung a long banner on the front of the bandstand proclaiming De Vargas and the Entrada to be a celebration of genocide against native peoples.

The Santa Fe Police had a massive presence on and around the Plaza. Chief Stuart himself had positioned his troops and then scurried back to the safety of the Washington Avenue station. He placed two cops at every street corner around the Plaza and outside the La Fonda Hotel and the First National Bank building. Got to protect the tourists and the bank. He stood with Antonio and seven other cops in their assigned places around the bandstand, directly across the street from the Palace of the Governors.

In addition, a large contingent of cops in riot gear waited on standby inside the Palace of the Governors courtyard in case they were needed. The Native Americans who normally would be selling their jewelry under the portico of the Palace of the Governors had abandoned their posts and gone back to their pueblos—or joined the protestors on the Plaza. The tourists had mostly cleared out, sensing trouble.

Up until the moment he heard drumming, he still harbored a smidgeon of hope that Ruben would call off the Entrada. That Ruben would do the right thing. The pounding of drums dashed his hopes. About a block up East Palace he saw two drummers leading the procession, followed by several foot soldiers carrying lances, long wooden spears with steel points. Behind the foot soldiers came two men on horseback, representing De Vargas and his chief lieutenant.

Not surprisingly, Ruben himself played the part of De Vargas with Larry Aragon as his lieutenant. An assortment of men and women supporters brought up the rear, none of them in costume. Some of them wore bicycle helmets, and some of them carried wooden nightsticks or other homemade weapons.

He sighed. "Here we go."

Antonio looked at him, irritated. "I still can't believe Ruben is this fucking stupid. We should have locked him up when we had the chance."

"For what?"

"For threatening to do this. We need to take these threats seriously. Act before they can be carried out."

"Good luck convincing the District Attorney."

As the procession came closer he noticed the period clothing worn by Ruben and Larry. They wore white shirts with puffy sleeves, black capes, and leather belts strapped diagonally across their chests that served as holsters for their swords. He recognized the thin blades of the Toledo swords that both men carried, no doubt originals from the sixteenth or seventeenth centuries, since he knew the Caballeros owned a good many antiquities from the conquistadores. The long thin blades could make a pincushion out of a human being. Both men wore the common Spanish helmet called a morion, which had a pronounced crest on top and sweeping sides that came to points in front and back.

Ruben and Larry rode slowly and proudly, erect in the saddle, crossing Washington Avenue and coming abreast of the Palace of the Governors.

Then the trouble started.

All at once a group of young protestors ran around the corner of Washington Avenue and began to hurl stones and bricks at the procession. A large rock struck one of the foot soldiers in the side of the head, knocking him to his knees and leaving a nasty gash above his temple. Dazed, he rested on his hands and knees bleeding onto the pavement.

Another rock hit Larry in the middle of the back. He pitched forward on the horse, which sent his helmet crashing to the pavement. Several of the foot soldiers scurried after the antique helmet trying to rescue it from the mob.

When one rock hit a cop in the chest, the cop picked up the fist-sized stone and hurled it back toward the protestors, now retreating to find more rocks.

Suddenly one of the protestors ran into the street and smacked Ruben's horse in the nose with his sign. The horse panicked and reared back, tossing Ruben onto the pavement. He landed flat on his back, knocking the wind out of him.

Struggling to roll over, Ruben groped for the sword underneath him. Before he could get to his hands and knees, the protestors attacked en masse, knocking Ruben over again and spooking his horse. The horse galloped off into the crowd trampling everyone in its path, protestors and Caballeros alike.

On the other horse Larry tried to kick his way free of the protestors, who pounded him with signs and grabbed at his legs. He managed to kick one protestor in the face before being pulled off the horse and plunging into the mob. He fought back, grabbing one of the protestors by the neck and punching him in the face before someone head-butted him and sent him crashing to the pavement. Meanwhile his horse, terrified, reared back and galloped off after Ruben's horse, leaving a trail of fallen bodies tossed like rag dolls on either side of Palace Avenue.

Now several protestors, including John Hammond, descended on one of the drummers. Hammond punched the man in the stomach, while someone else smacked him in the back with a sign. One of the protestors stomped on the man's drum, smashing it flat.

Responding to the protestors, the Entrada supporters with nightsticks counterattacked. They charged into the crowd swinging their clubs, but the protestors quickly encircled them, locking signs with nightsticks. Someone screamed, others shouted insults.

"Seal them off!" he shouted, realizing they would have to protect instead of arrest the Caballeros who were grossly outnumbered by the mob of protestors.

He and Antonio shoved their way into the street, coming between the two factions. One of the protestors made the mistake of hitting Antonio with his sign. Antonio grabbed the sign and broke it over his knee. Then the big man a grabbed the protestor by the shirt collar, picked him up, and tossed him like a paper doll into the crowd of peaceniks.

He didn't fare as well. When he turned to help a Caballero who had been struck by a rock, one of the protestors ran up and bashed him over the head with what felt like a nightstick. He crumpled to the pavement holding the back of his head. The next thing he knew he was sitting on his ass in the middle of the street watching a phantasmagoria of blurry shapes dancing across the pavement cursing and fighting with each other. All he could do was sit there on the pavement and wait for the moment to pass.

When his eyes began to focus, he saw Antonio holding one protestor around the neck and kicking another back into the crowd. Next to him Manny doubled over when an irate woman poked him in the stomach with a sign and then smacked him squarely on the head.

Just when it looked as though both the police and the Caballeros were about to be overwhelmed by the sheer number of protestors, the chief made the call to send in the riot police. They came pouring out of the Palace of the Governors with helmets and shields, swinging nightsticks at anyone who threatened them. The protestors surged back onto the Plaza, wanting nothing to do with the shielded cops and their nightsticks. It took only minutes for the riot police to literally shove and kick the last of the protestors off the street. Once finished, the riot police formed a line to protect the Caballeros and the fighting ended abruptly.

Now instead of fists, the protestors hurled insults and catcalls at the officers.

"Fuck the police!" one protestor shouted from the bandstand, mimicking the infamous NWA song.

"No more Entrada!" one woman screamed. "Don't celebrate genocide!"

"End colonialism!"

He spotted John Hammond sitting on the curb with blood dripping down his chin. The blood had stained his FIGHT THE POWER T-shirt bright red. He hobbled over to the curb and sat down beside Hammond, who looked like he'd taken a beating. In addition to a smashed nose, Hammond's ponytail had come loose during the melee and now hung down to his shoulders, a mop of dirty gray hair splattered with blood.

Hammond looked tired and haggard, like a seventy-year-old hippie who had just participated in one too many riots.

Hammond shook his head. "See, man, I told you it would get ugly. Why didn't you listen to me?"

"And I told you to stay out of it and no one would get hurt. Why didn't you listen to me?"

"Because you didn't keep the peace."

"No, *you* didn't keep the peace."

11

From his seat on the curb he watched the injured being helped into the Palace of the Governors. Inside a medical triage unit had been set up in the courtyard. One of the newer cops he didn't know helped Hammond across the street and into the Palace. When the cop came back for him, he refused assistance. He stood up stiffly and hobbled toward the double doors, wide open now to catch the weary and the wounded.

The medic inside directed him to a bench where Hammond and Ruben sat side by side, unlikely benchwarmers. He laughed at sight of them sitting together in sullen silence. Ruben looked as bad as Hammond, his face a mass of cuts and bruises. The two adversaries regarded each other with a mixture of embarrassment and distaste.

"Are you okay?" Antonio asked, coming up behind him.

"I'm still on my feet. What about you?"

Antonio grunted something unintelligible and went back outside to transport more of the injured.

He hobbled over to the bench occupied by Hammond and Ruben. Unable to resist, he sat down beside Ruben and joined the silent choir.

Ruben glared at him. "Don't say it. Leave me alone."

"I was hoping you'd come to your senses and call off the procession."

Hammond suddenly experienced a lucid moment. "Yeah, man, and abide by what you agreed to do...cancel the Entrada."

Ruben turned to Hammond. "You stay out of this. I know you. You're a damned hippie. You're one of those people who came in the seventies with all those other damned hippies. You have nothing to do with this conversation."

Hammond zoned out again, his eyes half closed.

Ruben sighed and turned back to him. "It's our tradition, man. Our culture. What the fuck?"

"And what did all this accomplish other than creating more ill will? Tell me? We have two dozen people injured, some seriously enough to be taken to the Emergency Room. For what? So you and your buddies can show off and pretend you didn't lose the argument?"

"You're just like Tito, a traitor to your people."

"That's bullshit!" he shot back, not about to listen to another lecture on the fucking People. "Tito and I were trying to represent ALL of Santa Fe, not just your little group of misfits. Wake up, the city has changed in the last decade."

"Maybe for you, but not for me and the people I represent."

He shook his head. "Then you'll have to live with the consequences. You're going to be cited for marching without a permit, and most likely for inciting a riot."

"Fuck off. I don't need your advice." Ruben stood up and hobbled off toward the door.

"We know where to find you."

"What an asshole," Hammond said after Ruben had gone.

He turned to Hammond angrily. "And you shut up."

Hammond started to apologize, but he ignored him, concentrating on a massive headache that pounded inside his skull.

While he waited for a medic to give him something for the headache, he watched Antonio drag in two more of the injured, one under each arm. One was a protestor, the other a Caballero. Both had head wounds. He shook his head in disgust, overwhelmed by how utterly ridiculous it was to be sitting here surrounded by the wounded from both camps.

Both sides needed to grow up and learn how to work together.

While he mused on the absurdity of the situation, the medics directed the more seriously wounded to cots set up in the courtyard until they could be transported to the Christus St. Vincent emergency room for stitches or X-rays. Most of the injuries required only cleaning and bandaging.

A few minutes later Chief Stuart breezed into the courtyard to check on the situation, still wearing his customary suit and tie. "Good work, men. We took care of that."

"We?" Antonio asked.

Stuart ignored Antonio. He came over to the bench. "What happened to you, Lopez?"

"Somebody hit me from behind. One of the protestors."

"Protestors? I thought these people were supposed to be peaceniks? The peace and love crowd?"

"Hah! You're forty years behind the times, Chief," Manny said from across the courtyard. "These people are mean motherfuckers."

Manny had one arm in a sling and a split lip.

"Well then...carry on," Stuart said and then breezed off, heading back to the station.

Manny waved goodbye, mocking the chief.

He just shook his head, glad to see Stuart leave them in peace.

He and Antonio waited until all the injured were treated or transferred to the Emergency Room and then limped back to the station together. The Plaza had emptied out. Only a few city workers remained to clean up the mess left behind by the rioters. Bloody bandages, torn clothing, smashed signs, rocks and wooden clubs littered Palace Avenue. Even horse shit.

"Manny checked out the people who sent Tito death threats," Antonio said as they walked side by side. "Turns out they all had alibis."

"So I heard. And from what I understand, all of them denied knowing anything about fifty caliber rifles."

"So what do you want me to do?"

He paused a moment outside the station to think. "I wonder. You were a former Marine. Do you know of any state or national registry for fifty caliber sniper rifles that would allow us to trace the one used by Tito's assassin? We think the gun may have been a Barrett."

Antonio shook his head. "There's no national registry. California has some sort of registry or special rules for fifty caliber weapons, but none of the other states do, as far as I know."

"I didn't think so."

Linda took one look at them and winced when they walked into the station. "I hope the other guys look as bad as you do."

He laughed, despite his headache.

Antonio shot her a dirty look. "Very funny."

On the way to his office he made a detour to their lunch room and picked up a cold pack, which he applied to the back of his head. After a few minutes of numbing relief, he returned the cold pack and considered his next move.

Sitting at his desk, he remembered A. J. Hoke. When Tommy called earlier, on his way out of town, he forgot to ask Baca about the dispute between Hoke and his neighbor, Robert Warner. If Hoke asked Tito to take his complaints to City Council at their September meeting, then the complaints must have been serious.

He checked his city calendar for the date of the September meeting. The Council was scheduled to meet on Wednesday of next week. If the agenda for the meeting had been compiled, it might include more information about Hoke's complaints.

He took out his city directory and called the Council Secretary, Betty Lucero.

"Betty, this is Detective Fernando Lopez calling."

"Fernando. Hi. I haven't talked to you in ages."

"I know. I've been too damn busy."

"So I hear. Sounds like you had your hands full on the Plaza this afternoon. What can I do for you?"

"Do you have the agenda ready for next week's meeting?"

"Yes, why do you ask?"

"I need to find out if Tito put an item on the agenda concerning the complaints of one A. J. Hoke. Hoke was having a dispute with his neighbor and wasn't happy with Tito's mediation. Apparently he asked Tito to take the issue to City Council."

There was a pause on the other end of the line. He could hear Betty shuffling papers. Then she returned.

"Okay, I have the agenda." She paused for a moment. "Tito's item is listed under New Business. I quote: 'A. J. Hoke complaint against neighbor, Robert Warner: noise, ordinance violation, possible illegal activity.'"

"That's all?"

"That's it. The agenda wouldn't include anything more than a one-line summary."

He thanked Betty. Before he could even hang up, he was thumbing through the Santa Fe phone directory for Hoke's number.

His mind raced: noise, ordinance violation, and possible illegal activity. What kind of illegal activity? Maybe he wasn't at a dead end after all.

He dialed the number.

12
Wednesday

The fresh morning air improved his mood as he turned onto Highway 41. Yesterday's massive headache had subsided into a stiff neck. He noticed the chamisa blooming yellow along the highway and behind it the smoky mesas receding in the distance. Last time he drove this highway he was too busy keeping up with Jodie to notice the beauty. He wondered if he should have waited until she could accompany him before interviewing Hoke. She happened to be occupied with a massive traffic accident on I-25 when he'd called this morning, so he decided to go solo. He could pass along whatever he learned to Jodie later this afternoon.

Hoke had agreed to a ten o'clock meeting and given him directions to his ranch. He drove by the spot where the young girl in the morgue had been murdered and past the three hills where the so-called treatment center was located. Soon the highway crossed over the Galisteo River bridge. The road then turned to the right in a long curve that brought him eventually to the Hoke Ranch, gated and fenced in with barbed wire.

He drove over the cattle guard and through the metal gate with "A. J. Hoke Ranch" displayed in prominent letters. His cruiser bounced over the gravel and crushed rock driveway that wound its way over the mesa to the ranch, a good quarter mile from the highway. Two border collies ran out to meet him and then followed him barking the rest of the way.

He pulled into to the gravel lot next to an old ranch house, a modest stone building with a porch shaded by a portico. He parked next to a classic 1950s Chevy pickup. The truck had long since faded to patches of blue-tinted rust. From his cruiser he could see a barn with a

John Deere tractor parked out front, a pump house, a chicken coop, and a series of corrals out back. In one of the corrals a few cattle gathered around the feeders, while outside on the mesa a herd of goats grazed on the open land.

From all appearances it was a working ranch.

When he tried to step out of his cruiser, the two border collies cornered him and growled suspiciously. "Good dogs," he said, squatting down on his knees and holding out his hand. The collies came over one at a time and sniffed him, then sidled up to allow him to stroke their backs. Soon they were all friends, at least for the moment.

He stood up, smelling the unmistakable odor of cow shit. Halfway to the porch he saw Hoke sitting under the portico watching him negotiate the two dogs. Hoke rose to his feet and walked out to meet him. He was a spry little man who looked to be in his late seventies, wearing boots and a western hat, with a pearl-button shirt hanging over his jeans.

Hoke held out his hand. "Pleased ta meetcha. About time they sent out some police to deal with them sonsabitches next door."

He laughed. "Well, not exactly."

"Come on up...have a seat in the shade,"

He followed him to the porch and took a seat on the bench next to Hoke. "So like I said in our phone conversation, I'm trying to figure out what's going on over there with your neighbors."

"Beats the hell out of me. I've lived here going on fifty years now, and I've never seen anything like that bunch. The guy who built that ranch about twenty years ago was bad enough. He was a Hollywood type, some sort of mogul or what have you, with lots of money and big ideas. Wanted to make it look like a glamorous Hollywood set, I guess. Can you imagine, in New Mexico? He would bring in all these starlets and such and throw wild parties all night long. Music so loud you could hear it all the way over here. Yeah, I've seen some of those starlets, they don't look like real people, if you know what I mean."

"No doubt. What about this new bunch? What were you were saying about them?"

"Hah! They're even worse. They're secretive and downright unfriendly. The guy who owns the place now comes and goes on a helicopter. Robert Warner's his name. He makes a hell of a noise with that helicopter. He comes and goes at all hours, day or night. Scares my livestock, even my chickens. The hens won't lay eggs anymore. But that's not all."

Hoke motioned behind the house. "All the land back there is BLM land, open range. I lease about a hundred sixty acres to graze my livestock. But those bastards next door shoot my cows and goats if they get too close to their land. And they must use a goddamned bazooka, because the animals are blown apart. Whatever they use, it's not a regular hunting rifle. And when I've gone over to talk to them, they tell me to get the hell off their land and mind my own business if I know what's good for me. Just like that. It's a threat."

"How many of your animals have they killed?"

Hoke stroked his unshaven face, deeply lined and burned almost black by the sun. "Far as I know, five or six. That's why I been keeping the cows in the corral lately."

"Did you tell Tito Garcia all this?"

"You bet I did. I contacted Tito because he'd helped me resolve my problems with the last owner of that ranch. Did a good job too. But this time, not so good. Tito seemed to be afraid of them. I wouldn't be surprised if they threatened him too. He got them to agree to cut the noise and wild parties and to stop shooting my livestock, none of which they actually did. I told Tito they'd gone back on their word but he said he couldn't do anything about it any more. Like I said, I think he was scared of them, especially the guy they call the Foreman."

"Yeah, I've met the Foreman."

Hoke shook his head. "Stay away from him. He's as mean as a rattlesnake."

"But Tito was going to take your complaints to the Santa Fe City Council, is that right? So he wasn't afraid to do that."

Hoke looked down at his lap. "Well, I reckon he was worried about something a little more serious. I don't even like to talk about it."

"You mean the young girls?"

Hoke turned away, as if embarrassed. "Dirty bastards. Warner brings in these rich guys, these big shots...he picks them up in his helicopter at the Santa Fe and Albuquerque airports. Brings them here to be with the girls."

"What do they do with the girls?"

"Hah! What do you think?"

"Just to be clear, we're talking about sex trafficking, right?"

Hoke glanced up at him and then whispered, "It's the devil's work. He's the devil incarnate, the Evil One."

He ignored Hoke's last statement, wanting to avoid bringing Satan into their conversation. "Where do the girls come from? How does Warner find them and bring them here?"

Hoke shook his head. "He brings them in on his helicopter. I don't know where the hell they come from, but one of them showed up here. She was trying to run away, half naked. She was crying like a baby. My wife thought she was thirteen or fourteen years old. She spoke Spanish, but it was a different kind of Spanish, Mexican Spanish or something. I could only understand a few words she said because she talked so fast. I mean, she was pretty near hysterical. But she kept saying one word I did understand, el encierro."

"Confinement or jail. How long ago was this?"

"Maybe a month, no more than that. But they were right behind her. She was only here for fifteen or twenty minutes. My wife didn't even have time to feed her. They pounded on the door until we opened it and then the big man, the Foreman, grabbed the girl by the hair. I mean, he drug her right out here on the porch and beat the living tar out of her. She was screaming so, I thought they were going to kill her right there on our porch."

"Did you call the sheriff?"

Hoke lowered his head. "No, sir, I did not. It's hard to get the sheriff out here...but that's not the real reason I didn't call. I'm ashamed to say I was afraid of them. I still am. Hell, if I were younger I'd get my shotgun and go over there and take care of business, I swear."

"No, you made the right decision to stay away, but you should have called the sheriff's office. We've found two young women murdered along Highway forty-one not far from here."

"Bastards," Hoke whispered.

"One of them may be the same girl who visited you."

"Maybe so. I really thought they were gonna kill her."

He slapped his knee. "So if I wanted to pay your neighbor a visit, how would I get there? Is there a driveway?"

"Good question. Like I said, they're secretive. They make it damn hard to find the place."

"So I noticed. I didn't see their driveway on my way here."

"Well, here's what you do. Go back to the highway and head north, the way you came down. Just on the other side of the Galisteo River there's a dirt road heading west. It takes you down to the riverbed, which is bone dry most of the year. You'll see tire tracks when you get down there. Follow the riverbed west for about half a mile. You'll come to a gravel road off to your right that will take you into the ranch. You can't miss the road because it goes up between two rock formations. That's the entrance to the ranch."

"Thanks. I think I might take a look before I head back to Santa Fe."

"But be careful...these people are dangerous."

Just then Mrs. Hoke came out on the porch carrying two glasses of iced tea. "I thought you boys might like a cold drink," she said, a tall thin woman with kindly eyes and gray hair braided to her waist.

"Thank you, that's very kind of you. Feels like it's going to be another hot afternoon."

Hoke nodded. "Yes it is. And getting hotter."

He wasn't sure Hoke was talking about the weather.

Part Two: Three-Hills Ranch

13

She waited until everyone was asleep and the guard had left for the night. Then she slipped out of the sheets and grabbed her robe and flip-flops, the only shoes they were allowed. Silently she tip-toed over to the next cubicle to rendezvous with Antonia to carry out their escape plan. She heard snoring from the other side of the bunkhouse and someone nearby crying in the dark. She bent down over Antonia's bed and tugged on her sheet.

"Antonia, are you ready?"

She felt Antonia shaking underneath the sheet, which she had pulled up tight under her chin.

Antonia sobbed. "I can't…I'm too scared…you go on by yourself."

"Please, come with me. They'll kill you here, like the others. I need you."

Antonia pulled the sheet over her head. "I can't. Leave me alone."

Now she didn't know what to do. Should she wait and try to enlist someone else to come with her? She glanced back at her cubicle. No, tonight was the full moon she'd waited for. In the moonlight she could see the trail that would take her out of the hills to the highway, where she could hitchhike a ride or walk if she had to all the way to Santa Fe. She had to take a chance. If she stayed here they would kill her.

She tied the robe around her waist and carrying her flip-flops made her way to the rear door, away from the big house where her captors were sleeping. Before leaving she stepped into the bathroom and pulled her long dark hair back in a ponytail and put a rubber band around it. Outside, she slipped into her flip-flops and walked through the yard, trying to stay within the shadows of the outbuildings.

Every few paces she stopped to listen for the Foreman, the one she feared the most. He sometimes patrolled at night. They could hear him outside walking around the buildings to make sure none of them were outside after their eight o'clock curfew--unless they were servicing one of clients in which case they sometimes wouldn't return until early morning.

Tonight she heard nothing, only the lonely howl of a coyote behind the hills. Only when she found the trail did she begin to run, slowly at first and then faster the further she ran. She stopped when she came to the hill and listened to make sure the Foreman wasn't following her. Then she began climbing the steep hill in small quick steps, using the breathing techniques she had learned back home to outrun the men who tried to rape her, or worse.

Halfway to the top the trail divided, one path going to the summit and the other going around the hill toward the highway. She took the path to the highway, struggling to keep her flip-flops on her feet as she ran. Finally she stopped and removed the flimsy shoes and held them tightly in her hand while running. The moon overhead bathed the sagebrush ahead in a silvery light that would have frightened her if she wasn't running away from something even more frightening back at the ranch.

When the moon went behind a cloud, the mesa plunged into momentary darkness. She waited until her eyes adjusted and then proceeded more carefully as she made her way through clumps of cactus and sagebrush, the needles and branches scratching her legs and piercing her bare feet. She stopped when she heard a sound up ahead and saw branches of chamisa moving in the shadows. A small animal, she thought. Rabbit or coyote or maybe one of the herd of goats that grazed on the mesa.

She came finally to a slab of rock, a huge boulder buried in the ground with a flat surface on which she could rest. She sat down and then laid back on the rock, still warm from the late summer sun. Tears streamed down her face as she began feeling the pain on the bottoms of her feet, the flesh ripped and torn and covered in blood.

She'd made it this far without being seen. Another half-mile and she would be on the highway, where she could hitch a ride to freedom.

She'd dreamed of this moment from day they'd brought her to the ranch three months ago. The thought of finally being free of them re-energized her. She scrambled to her feet and climbed down from the rock and walking now continued on toward the highway.

Straight ahead she could see the faint ribbon of the highway. So close and yet so far away. She heard a car in the distance coming toward her and then saw its lights splash on the highway as it rounded a bend in the road and roared off heading south toward the town of Galisteo.

If only she had been quicker, she thought. She could be in that car now moving away from this nightmare. But there would be other cars, she told herself. All she had to do was make it down to the highway. So she ignored the pain in her feet and the scratches on her legs and moved on through the bushes, never taking her eyes from the highway.

The barbed wire fence surprised her. Watching the highway, she had not noticed the fence. The barbs tore through her thin robe and undergarments when she bumped into the fence. She searched for a place to cross, finding a spot where a heavy log had been placed over the lower strand of wire. She held the top strand and stepped through the opening to the other side of the fence.

Now she found herself in a wide ditch or ravine running along the highway. She struggled with her footing across the damp, squishy ground still wet from the last rain. Just as she climbed the bank to the side of the road she heard a car approaching from the south and then saw its lights flickering in the distance as it crested one small hill after another. She almost jumped for joy.

Freedom!

A burst of adrenaline picked her up and carried her up onto the shoulder of the highway. She waved and jumped up and down, no longer feeling the shooting pain in her feet.

The car was slowing down. The driver had seen her on the side of the highway and was stopping to help her! She'd done it. Her plan had worked.

She continued to wave as the car came slowly out of the darkness into focus until she saw that it was the jeep, the Foreman's jeep at the ranch. She cursed at him and at herself for thinking she could escape. How stupid she'd been.

She almost collapsed on the pavement, her spirits plunging. But fear overcame her. She was afraid of what he would do to her, the many ways he tortured and killed them when they resisted. She'd seen him kill Maria. How many more had he killed?

Sobbing now, she turned and tried to run away from them on the shoulder of the highway. She heard the car swerve onto the shoulder behind her and then the bright headlights swallowed her. She screamed as the force of the jeep struck her from behind and crushed her underneath.

Pain. Voices. Darkness.

14
Wednesday

From the bridge the Galisteo River looked as dry as Death Valley, a white ribbon of sand and rock stretching out to the horizon. Not a trace of water or mud anywhere. Still, he worried the river bottom would be too deep for the cruiser, never great in an off-road situation. So he eased the car down into the riverbed and tried to drive on the far right edge of the sand, allowing him to keep two wheels on solid ground. Like this he made his way slowly down the river until he saw the two rock formations on the right bank. Just as Hoke said, a gravel road ran from the riverbed up to a flat parking area and then continued on between the twin towers of red sandstone.

He parked off to one side, where the cruiser would not be visible from the ranch. He took his binoculars out of the glove compartment and made his way through the opening in the rocks. The road ran straight ahead to the top of a small rise on which stood the guardhouse. Only the roofs of the other buildings were visible over the rise. He needed to climb higher in order to get a better view of these buildings and the layout of the valley.

Returning to the cruiser, he walked along the base of the rock formation looking for a way to the top. Farther down he found a ravine created by water running off the cliff into a crevice. The crevice provided a stairway of sorts that allowed him to climb slowly rock by rock to the top. From his position, about fifty feet high, he could see the entire ranch.

Never in his wildest imagination could he have envisioned a property this opulent in the middle of the New Mexico desert. The house alone would have cost tens of millions of dollars with its four separate wings and elaborate courtyard, not to mention the tower at its southeastern corner.

Conspicuous consumption at its worst, he thought as he looked out on the helipad behind the house and the wooden barracks at the far end of the valley. He counted three Range Rovers parked side by side near the house, but the helipad was empty at the moment.

He settled into a sitting position, watching with his binoculars for any movement. He thought he could make out the shadow of someone in the guardhouse, possibly the Foreman. A few minutes later he saw two young women being escorted by a man walk out of the barracks. They strolled over to a nearby gazebo and took seats on a shady bench under its roof. The man escorting them sat on the opposite side of the gazebo. Like the Foreman, he was wearing a khaki uniform and baseball cap. The three of them sat in silence for about fifteen minutes and then walked back to the barracks. Not one word was spoken.

He lowered the binoculars in order to rest his eyes, but as he did he saw the same man escort two different young women out of the barracks and walk them to the gazebo. The first two women—or girls really—had brown skin and dark hair. From a distance they looked Hispanic to him. The second set had lighter, olive skin. One of them had brown hair, and the other blond. Like the first group, they sat on the bench without speaking for about fifteen minutes and then were escorted back to the barracks by the man in khaki.

Just as the man in khaki came out with two more young women he heard the rattling sound of a helicopter approaching. He ducked down behind a boulder. He watched the copter circle around from the north and then hover over the helipad for a few seconds, leveling. Then it descended slowly, touching down in a windstorm of dust and dead tumbleweeds. The copter looked to him like a blue-and-white striped Sikorsky, one of the company's more expensive models.

A friend who owned Southwestern Air Tours had told him the Sikorsky copters were the safest on the market.

And expensive, like everything else at Three-Hills Ranch.

While he watched, the blades of the helicopter chugged to a stop. Three men climbed out of the cabin, including one older man wearing a blue suit with no tie. He assumed that would be Robert Warner. The other two wore jeans and polo shirts and carried duffel bags. The three of them ducked and headed toward a door in the rear of the house.

The pilot stayed behind, another man dressed all in khaki. He climbed out later and made his rounds inspecting the engine and the rotors. Finished, he closed the doors of the copter and then walked off to join the others in the big house.

He waited a few minutes and then decided to leave. He could do nothing else today, but they would be back soon enough with a search warrant. Jodie had promised to take care of that.

He stood up and paused a moment to stretch his cramping legs. Before he could move he heard a sound he recognized. Crack! A rock in front of him exploded, showering him with fragments of stone. They stung his face and brought tears to his eyes. Reeling, he stumbled back and lost his balance. He tried to grab hold of the boulders along the side as he fell and then slid over the loose rocks in the crevice. He hit bottom with a jolt to his spine. Ignoring his scratched and bleeding hands, he quickly got to his feet and looked around.

He assumed the shooter must have seen him from the guardhouse and would probably come after him. He needed to get out of here fast.

An adrenaline rush sent him scrambling to his cruiser. He climbed into the driver's seat and hit the ignition. Then he took off fast down the riverbank and hit the sand spinning. When he came out of the spin he hit the accelerator hard, trying to wipe his hands on his shirt as he drove. No time for caution now as he raced down the riverbed toward the bridge. He kept checking his rear view mirror until he finally saw an ATV pop into view.

"Fuck!" he said out loud, knowing what was coming next. He ducked down low in the seat as he approached the bridge, bouncing up over the riverbank and finally onto Highway 41. He'd gone only a hundred feet or so on the pavement when he heard the Crack! The bullet clunked against the rear of the cruiser. He tensed, worried the car might burst into flames at any second. But nothing happened. He stomped on the accelerator and didn't ease up until the speedometer hit ninety mph.

Only when he came to the intersection of highways 41 and 285 did he start to relax. The ATV wouldn't be able to follow him on a major highway like 285, not at this speed.

About halfway to Santa Fe he decided to pull over and check the damage. He found a flat pull-off where county highway workers had stored a mound of gravel for the upcoming winter.

When he stopped and climbed out of the cruiser he saw a gaping hole in the left rear fender. Fortunately, the bullet had missed the gas tank. Standing there he noticed approaching cars were beginning to slow down. Some of them even stopped. It took a moment for him to realize why. Here he stood with blood on his shirt alongside a cop car with a gaping bullet hole in its rear fender: the kind of sight that attracted the curious and the voyeuristic.

One young woman driving a bright red Mini pulled up and lowered her car window. "Excuse me, sir. Do you need help?"

"No, I'm fine."

Then a man parked his pickup near the gravel mound and walked over to help. "Do you need a lift to the ER?"

He waved them away. "I'm fine! I just had a little fall while hiking. I'm on my way home now."

Both of them looked suspiciously at the bullet hole. "Whatever you say, officer," the man said and walked off.

The incident irritated him. He hated to look like a damned fool, which he surely did at the moment.

Back on the road, he took the last Santa Fe exit and headed home to clean up before reporting for duty at the station. Fortunately Estelle was gone when he pulled into their driveway on Acequia Madre. What she didn't know wouldn't hurt her. He went inside, tore off his shirt, and stuffed it in the kitchen garbage can. Then he headed for the bathroom, where he washed his face and hands with an antiseptic soap that made his hands sting so bad he let out a howl of rage.

His face wasn't so bad. It just looked like he'd nicked himself a few times while shaving. He could live with that.

Finished, he grabbed a bottle of cold water from the refrigerator and headed out to the cruiser thinking the day could not possibly get any worse. That notion lasted all of five minutes.

As soon as he turned on Washington Avenue he saw what looked like every police car, fire truck, and ambulance in the city of Santa Fe parked around the Plaza. What now?

He parked and set the brake. He ran into the station and found it deserted except for Linda at the front counter and the chief pacing back and forth in the long hallway muttering to himself.

"What's going on here?"

Both Linda and the chief stared at him in disbelief.

"You mean you haven't heard?" the chief asked. "The Indians have occupied the Palace of the Governors."

"It's sixteen eighty all over again," Linda added.

He stood at the front counter confused. "Indians?"

The chief waved him off. "Okay, the Pueblos, you know who I mean. To get even with the Caballeros for staging the Entrada and celebrating the Reconquest, they're claiming to have re-enacted the Pueblo Revolt of sixteen eighty. You know, when they united to take over all the government buildings and drive the Spanish out of Northern New Mexico."

"Come on, you can't be serious." He didn't know what else to say. He couldn't believe Henry Ortiz and the All Pueblo Council of Governors could be as stupid as Ruben and his posse.

"It's true, and we don't know if the Pueblos are armed or what. Rumor has it that Ruben and some of the Caballeros are on their way downtown to take back the Palace by force. We have to stop this before it gets out of hand. Both sides have gone crazy!"

"I don't believe Henry would allow guns in the Palace. Or Ruben, for that matter."

The chief shouted: "Who knows? Like I said, they're all crazy!"

"What happened to your face?" Linda asked calmly, in contrast to the volatile Stuart, who continued his pacing.

In the confusion he had forgotten about his face. "It's a long story. I'll explain later."

He headed for the door, leaving Linda to try and calm the chief. Good luck with that.

From the parking lot he could see the crunch of emergency vehicles surrounding the Plaza. Inside the circle of vehicles the Department had set up A-Frame barricades blocking access to the Palace of the Governors. A large crowd of onlookers had gathered beyond the barriers, including a group of Native American singers and dancers who were performing on East Palace. On West Palace supporters of the Caballeros were hurling insults and threats to both the Native Americans and the Police for protecting the Native American occupiers. The dueling groups cancelled each other out and produced a deafening hum as he walked through the police lines onto the Plaza.

He spotted Manny and Antonio standing beside the main door to the Palace of the Governors. He joined them under the portico. Antonio threw up his arms in disgust. "Look at this mess! I tell you, we should have arrested Ruben when we had the chance, before the trouble started."

"He's been cited for organizing a parade without a permit. You can't keep a man in jail for that."

"What about inciting a riot."

"The district attorney hasn't made a decision on that."

Antonio laughed. "Fine, but every hour more people on both sides of the issue are arriving. We've talked to Puebloans from as far away as Taos and Isleta. Caballeros supporters are coming up from Socorro and Albuquerque. All the cowboys and Indians are just aching for a fight! Look at them! You'd think it was sixteen eighty all over again!"

He nodded, well aware of the cultural dynamics. He knew history was an open wound in places like Santa Fe where three distinct cultures had coexisted—sometimes peacefully, and sometimes not—for five hundred years. The end result was a lot of resentment on all sides. The Puebloans resented the Hispanics for their original invasion beginning with Coronado in 1540 and especially for their return or Entrada in 1692. The Hispanics resented the Puebloans for their rebellion in 1680.

And the Anglos? The Anglos resented everyone who was here before them.

"It's an open wound, history. Lots of resentment," he said.

"Yeah, well it's time to move beyond the resentment."

"We miss Tito," Manny added. "He was the one person who could bring the two sides together. The one city leader who everyone trusted."

"Not everyone. Don't forget, Tito was murdered."

Manny looked at him and frowned.

"So tell me what happened this morning. Was there a provocation? An incident?"

Antonio shook his head. "No provocation. The Indians showed up about eight o'clock as always and pretended to set up shop. Then when the doors opened at nine, they all rushed in at the same time and forced the museum staff out. We think there's about twenty of them inside, maybe a few more. Every so often a couple of their supporters break through the barricades and try to join them, but so far we've managed to keep out most of the newcomers. If the entire crowd rushes us at the same time, then we're gonna be in big trouble."

"Who's in charge inside?"

"Good question. As far as we can tell it's Henry Ortiz, the head of the All Pueblo Council of Governors. We know he's inside because he's the one who announced that they were taking over the Palace and reenacting the sixteen eighty Rebellion."

"Have you tried to speak with him?"

"We've knocked on the door several times, but there's been no response from Henry or anyone else."

"I'm not worried about Henry so much. I'm more worried about Ruben and his posse. Chief says there's a rumor that Ruben's getting his guys together and plans to make an armed raid on the Palace."

"We've heard the same thing."

"We can't let that happen." He walked over to the massive front doors on the Palace and pounded on the heavy wood.

Both Antonio and Manny moved to the side so as not to be seen if the door should open.

He pounded again. "Henry Ortiz! It's Fernando Lopez! Open the door so we can talk!"

One of the heavy doors opened slightly. A woman who he didn't recognize poked her head around the door and said, "He will only talk to your mayor. Go send for him. Knock again when he arrives."

The door slammed closed in his face, leaving him frustrated and irritated at the thought of having to go fetch Joe Martin, the mayor, who was a newcomer to the city and had absolutely no understanding or experience dealing with these intractable groups.

Still, he followed her orders. He sent Manny to City Hall to fetch the mayor. "Tell Martin that Henry will only talk to him. And that it's urgent, we need him to come right now."

While they waited, he and Antonio watched the crowd for signs of impending violence. They noticed the crowd had grown more restless. By evening events could easily spin out of control. One spark, one stupid act of aggression could ignite a firestorm that would be impossible to put out without backup from neighboring cities like Albuquerque or even the National Guard. If a crowd of people started shooting, the Santa Fe Police Department would need a lot of help.

They didn't have long to wait, because Manny and Joe Martin came running down Lincoln Avenue together. Fernando actually liked Martin, a short balding man who always dressed in the finest Santa Fe Chic: jeans, white shirt, and blue jacket, with a heavy turquoise bolo tie. What bothered him was that Martin was just getting his bearings in a city steeped in history and cultural conflict. At the moment Santa Fe needed someone who understood the nuances of the conflict. Santa Fe needed someone like Tito.

"What's the situation?" Martin asked, gasping for air.

He explained the situation as best he could in sixty seconds. "Henry Ortiz says he will only talk to you."

"Are they armed?"

"Not that we know of."

"Okay, then let's do this." Martin walked over to the door and knocked hard. He waited patiently until the door opened and the same woman appeared. "Who are you?" she asked Martin.

Martin was taken aback. "Who are you?"

He had to laugh at that. It was a perfect cross-cultural moment. The woman had no idea who the mayor of Santa Fe was. She lived in a nearby pueblo with its own governor. As for Martin, he didn't have a clue about the identity of the woman.

Martin introduced himself as the mayor of Santa Fe and waited for her to open the door. When she did, he disappeared quickly into the depths of the Palace.

Antonio walked off to the La Fonda Hotel to find a restroom, while he waited. He scanned the crowd, looking for Ruben. Everything seemed calm at the moment, as long as Ruben and his posse didn't appear.

Antonio returned a few minutes later complaining about the

lack of facilities on the Plaza. He ignored him, waiting for Martin to reappear. When he did it was clear from the look on his face that his meeting with Henry had not been pleasant—or successful.

Martin shook his head. "What a pompous ass. We didn't even talk. He just lectured me on being a newcomer and not knowing anything about the deep history of Santa Fe. I quote him directly: 'who are you to speak with me...my people have been here for a thousand years' and so on. Christ, you can't even have a civil conversation with these people!"

"These people?"

"You know what I mean."

Just then the heavy doors to the Palace creaked open and the same woman appeared. She waved at Martin to come back to the entrance.

Martin shuffled back to the door, apprehensive.

"Henry Ortiz will only speak with one of your elders. He wants to speak with Fernando Lopez."

"Great, so I'm an elder now," he said to Antonio, who shrugged.

Martin waved him over.

"Follow me." The woman led him into the Palace, making sure to close and lock the door behind them.

As soon as he stepped inside he smelled smoke, the scent of piñon wood burning in the corner fireplaces. Drums beat slowly in the background. The Puebloans had moved tables and heavy furniture into the front room, presumably to use as barricades. He saw at least a dozen of them lounging around, waiting for what would happen next. None of them carried weapons or looked particularly militant. Most sat on the floor reading or smoking or talking in small groups. He knew only one, Russell Tso from Tesuque Pueblo, the son of an enjarrar who had repaired a kiva fireplace at his house two years ago.

Henry sat on a bench in the courtyard, where the city had brought those wounded during Tuesday's Entrada riot, including him and Ruben. He wore a beaded leather vest with a red bandana tied around his gray hair. Henry smiled when he saw him.

"Henry, I have come to make peace."

"'Bout time...after four hundred years."

He laughed.

"You're the only white man I trust, now that Tito's gone. You're a good man. You've always done the right thing."

"It's true, we've known each other a long time."

Henry nodded, moving over on the bench to make room for him. "So what happened with the Entrada? We worked on that for months with Tito and the Caballeros and all the other groups. We agreed to cancel it for the good of the community and because it was an affront to Native peoples. We don't have a Fiesta parade celebrating our Rebellion, so why should the Caballeros have one celebrating the Reconquest? You see the problem?"

He took a seat beside Henry. "I do see the problem, but remember, this was not an official procession sponsored by the Caballeros. It was a rogue event organized by Ruben Ortega and his posse."

Henry pondered what he had said. "Yes, but what difference does it make, finally? The Entrada was still performed in front of the Fiesta crowd in violation of our agreement. We all agreed to cancel this and any other celebration of violence in Santa Fe."

"You're right, we should have stopped it. At the time we worried that if we tried to arrest them in front of hundreds of people on the Plaza, including their supporters, we would cause a riot in the city. Ironically, not stopping them also caused a riot. So we found ourselves in a tough place. If it's any consolation, Ruben and his posse have been cited for what they did. For both conducting a parade without a permit and possibly inciting a riot."

Henry nodded. "Good. Here, let me show you something."

He followed Henry into the dimly-lit interior of the Palace of the Governors.

"Look at this." Henry pointed to a glass window over a cut-out section of the original adobe wall built in the early 1600s. The adobes had been burned black by fire long ago.

"My people burned these adobes three hundred and forty years ago, after we took back what was ours. My people's presence here goes back thousands of years. Why should we let these newcomers wipe out our history with theirs?"

He sighed. "I don't know, Henry. Sometimes I think history is a trap. It's like quicksand. It can swallow you alive. If you're stuck in the past, like so many of us in Santa Fe, you can't exist in the present. You see what I mean?"

Henry did not respond. Instead, he regarded him for several seconds and then nodded his head. "I hear you."

"So how do we make peace now, Henry. How do we get you to leave the Palace?"

"You tell me. You're the peacemaker. You and Tito."

"Okay, how about this? The Caballeros agree to not stage the Entrada in the future, and you agree to leave the Palace and not stage the Rebellion going forward? Quid pro quo."

Henry shook his head. "We already agreed to that. How's that going to stop Ruben Ortega or someone else, maybe one of his posse, from organizing another Entrada?"

"What if we put it in writing and have Ruben sign the agreement? We can also advertise that anyone organizing or participating in the Entrada—or the Rebellion—will automatically be charged with inciting a riot?"

Henry smiled. He considered the proposal.

"Yeah, that might work...let me run it by my people and get back to you. I should have an answer by this evening or tomorrow morning at the latest. I'll send you a text."

That made him laugh. "That's funny. We've come from smoke signals to texts and we still can't get along."

"It's true, my friend. We haven't learned a damned thing about getting along with one another."

"Maybe we can change that. For Tito."

"For Tito."

They shook hands, and then the same woman as before escorted him to the door. She locked and bolted it behind him without saying a word.

Outside the sunset had painted the western sky crimson and purple. He didn't see Manny or Antonio anywhere on the street. Most of the crowd had already dispersed, as had the emergency vehicles surrounding the Plaza. Only a small police squad remained, manning the barricades across the street from the Palace. He walked back to the station in the semi-darkness and then, after checking with the night dispatcher, headed home to Estelle.

15

When he walked exhausted into their kitchen, Estelle greeted him exactly as he knew she would. She said, "Why didn't you call, I've been worried!" And then she gave him a big hug. They were still affectionate after forty years of marriage, inseparable really, except when it came to going to church every Sunday morning and her other church activities. And his work, of course. She understood that he had to perform his duties as a police detective, but she never let him forget that he needed to keep her informed, in touch.

He held her at arms length and admired her petite, youthful look. Not even her streaked gray hair could diminish the fact that she looked much younger than he did. His colleagues at the station often commented on his wrinkled face, as wrinkled as a saguaro cactus was the standing joke. Too much sun, too many worries. Estelle on the other hand had few wrinkles on her face, being someone who was careful to avoid too much sun and who used sunscreen religiously. True, he was careless about the little things like sunscreen, he just never seemed to have the time to worry about such matters. Instead, he worried about the big things—like stress, for example, which was inescapable in his profession.

He sighed. "Sorry, it's been a crazy day. You won't believe the latest new from the Entrada wars."

He walked into their living room and slumped down in his personal lazy boy recliner. Estelle followed, bringing him a Santa Fe Pale Ale. She took a seat on the other side of a small side table in her own recliner. He saw she had a glass of white wine for herself. "Cheers," he said.

"So what's the latest?"

"Well, Henry Ortiz and his followers have occupied—that is, taken over—the Palace of the Governors in what they're calling a re-enactment of the Pueblo Revolt of sixteen eighty."

Estelle stared at him. "You're kidding, right?"

"I wish. He says if Ruben Ortega and his people can stage the Reconquest, they can stage the Revolt. Tit for tat."

Estelle clucked her tongue, which she normally did when she didn't approve of something. "Let me guess, all Ruben and Henry's followers are male, am I right about that?"

He grinned, knowing what was coming. "Yeah, pretty much."

"Well, what's wrong with you?" she said, a statement more than a question, and took her glass of wine back to the kitchen.

He knew she was referring to his gender more than to him personally, even though in her view he probably fit the mold as well as Ruben or Henry or any other male he could name.

He'd kept her informed about Tito's assassination and the ongoing war over the Entrada, including the Tuesday riot. What he hadn't told her about was the situation at Three-Hills Ranch, the two dead girls and Warner's alleged sex-trafficking of young women. He'd kept all that to himself, knowing it would upset Estelle terribly. She would imagine herself as the mother of those murdered girls. Worse, she would imagine their daughters Flavia and Adela as the victims, just as he had done in his nightmare. Why burden her with such depressing thoughts? She was better off not knowing about Three-Hills.

Estelle called from the kitchen. "Dinner's ready."

Over dinner they swapped stories about their day. She told him her Saint Francis Outreach Program had located another church willing to temporarily house as many as twenty immigrants. He gave her more information about the stand-off at the Palace. These quiet moments with Estelle always made him feel lucky. They had done well together, especially considering how young they were when they married, Estelle only nineteen and him twenty, high school sweethearts. But they had been good for each other, as sentimental as that sounded. He'd never for one moment regretted their youthful decision to marry and spend their lives together.

For the first few years of their marriage he worked part-time at Johnson's Lumber Yard and took classes at UNM, majoring in Criminal Justice. When Flavia was born, their first child, he dropped out of UNM and entered the Santa Fe Police Academy. Not only did he need a full-time job to support the family, he decided that instead of studying Criminal Justice he would rather work in the field. Those early years in the SFPD were the hardest, because back then he and the other young Chicanos were treated like second-class citizens. Ironic, since he and many of the others were from Santa Fe's oldest families. But he learned to swallow his pride and hold his tongue. He learned to accept the shit assignments.

Yes, he had paid his dues. Big time.

After dinner he washed the dishes and put them away. Then they made tea and went out on the back patio to enjoy the warm evening, with fireflies sparkling in the cottonwoods along the acequia and a three-quarters moon hanging in the night sky. The smell of a Santa Fe autumn was in the air tonight, that whiff of piñon and ponderosa pine that he so loved. Not many people knew that Santa Fe was located at an altitude of 7,200 feet, so there was always that scent of mountain pine in the air.

Eventually Estelle went back inside to watch television or listen to the music on KUNM, her favorite ways to relax in the evening. He stayed outside on the patio for a while, ruminating on how he always felt a sense of relief when he stepped inside their small adobe, where they had lived since early in their marriage. Stress from work seemed to melt away the instant he walked through their front door.

Their house might be small by today's standards, but it had been big enough to raise two children back in his day, before the rich Anglos from New York and Los Angeles moved to Santa Fe and remodeled the old adobes on streets like Acequia Madre into ten and twenty room mansions. He took great pride in the fact that he had preserved the original look of his adobe, built in the 1920s. He couldn't care less that their house had become something of an eyesore to many of his wealthy neighbors. Anyway, the crumbling adobe wall around their house and back patio prevented the nouveau Santa Feans from bothering them.

He was deep in thought when Estelle came out to get him. "You have a phone call, Fernando," she announced.

He followed her inside to the phone but did not recognize the voice. "Detective Lopez, this is Delores Ruiz, Tito's sister. I've been going through Tito's affairs and wanted to give you a report."

"Okay."

"I read Tito's will today with his lawyer. Tito left his house and personal estate to me. His business he left to Tommy Baca with the hope that Tommy would take over his mediation practice. I think that's good. I like Tommy, and I think he'll do a wonderful job."

She paused for a moment. "The thing is, Tito's death has made me reflect on my own life. To make a long story short, I've decided to sell my house in L.A. and move back to Santa Fe. I want to live here...in Tito's house. I love the idea of living next to national forest land. Besides, life is short, as I'm sure you of all people would know. So I'm going to follow my instincts."

He wasn't sure what she meant by 'you of all people would know.'

She continued. "In a sense I'll be coming home. Tito and I grew up in Santa Fe, even though we were born in Española. Funny, after all these years I still think of Santa Fe as my home."

"I understand. I've never felt at home anywhere else."

"This brings me to a question I wanted to ask you. What do you think I should do for Tito's service? You knew him better than I did. What kind of service do you think he would want?"

"Mrs. Ruiz, I really don't think I'm the right person to ask. That's a decision you should make as the nearest of kin."

"Well, here's what I'm thinking. I thought a memorial service at Saint Francis Auditorium would be nice. Not a funeral, a memorial service where people who knew Tito could share their memories. Tito wasn't religious, but he loved that auditorium in the Museum of Art. When we were kids, we would hold hands and walk down East Palace together to the museum. I remember, we both loved looking at the murals."

He heard her gently weeping at the other end. "I'm sorry for your loss, Mrs. Ruiz."

"Forgive me for intruding on you like this. I just wish I'd stayed closer to Tito. If only I could do it over again...but I guess we don't get do-overs in life, do we."

"No, sadly we don't."

"Well, thank you. I will keep you posted about the service. I don't have a date yet, but I'm looking at next Tuesday."

"I appreciate that." He hung up the phone.

He wished he could do something to lessen her grief—offer more consolation, bring back Tito from the dead. Something.

What was the old saying?

"If wishes were horses, beggars might ride."

16
Thursday

He sat at his desk enjoying his second cup of coffee and the morning light reflecting down the hallway to his office. He'd reported for work early again today, hoping to resolve the stand-off on the Plaza. If they could persuade Ruben to forego the Entrada going forward, they could persuade Henry and his people to leave the Palace of the Governors peacefully. He expected Ruben to be the problem, so he and Chief Stuart had worked out a deal whereby if Ruben would agree to the elimination of the Entrada they would drop the inciting a riot charge. Ruben would only have to pay a fine for parading without a permit, which didn't amount to much more than a slap on the wrist.

While he mused, the phone rang. "Fernando, this is Jodie Williams," the familiar voice said. "I should have the search warrant by this afternoon. It's been hell getting the judge to agree. I tell you this Robert Warner guy is well connected. I had to provide the judge with tons of evidence just to establish probable cause. Warner's lawyer is already throwing around his weight."

"I'm not surprised, Warner's filthy rich."

"Yeah, we've initiated a background check on him. He's a high roller from Hollywood who lives most of the year in Vegas. He has a mansion on the Strip and supposedly a production company somewhere in Vegas. He's independently wealthy, dabbles in producing films, you can imagine what kind of films, and no one seems to know where or how he gets his money. A slippery character."

"Thanks. We've been so busy with this Entrada business and the protests here that we haven't had the time to do much with Warner. I did interview Hoke at his ranch the other day, though. He told me where to find the entrance to Three-Hills Ranch, so I helped myself to a look around. I got quite a reception. I'll tell you all about it later."

"Okay, I'll call you later on your cell when I have more news about the search warrant."

He hung up the phone, grabbed his coffee, and headed for the chief's office for a morning briefing. He took one step into the hallway before his phone rang again. His first impulse was to ignore the phone, but then a sense of duty kicked in and he changed his mind and returned to his desk.

"Fernando! This is Tommy Baca!"

He detected a note of hysteria in Tommy's voice that seemed out of character for the usually calm young man.

"I'm sorry to bother you like this, but we need your help. We're being pursued by the same people who killed Tito. They've been following us since we left Santa Fe...and they're outside waiting for us now. Can you help us? Please! I don't know what else to do!"

"Okay, calm down, Tommy. First of all, where are you? And second, who are you with?"

"We're in the hotel at Buffalo Thunder...you know, the casino in Pojoaque. I thought we'd be safe somewhere with lots of people around, but they followed us anyway, they're waiting outside."

He was familiar with Buffalo Thunder, having spent a few evenings losing money at the Black Jack tables along with some of his colleagues. The casino was about ten miles due east of Santa Fe on Highway 285. It was an easy, ten-minute drive.

"I'm with Ana, the woman who was living in Tito's guesthouse. I'll tell you about her later. Sorry if I haven't been more forthcoming, but I've been scared of these people. They murdered Tito."

"Okay, what room are you in?"

"We're in room three-five-two...but be careful, they're driving a blue and white Range Rover."

"How many of them are there?"

"Two guys, both dressed in khaki with baseball caps, you can't miss them."

"I'm on my way."

He decided to skip his meeting with the chief now that he had a legitimate excuse. He would explain later if and when the chief had a civil moment. That was becoming his mantra: he would explain later.

When Antonio didn't answer his cell phone, he made the decision to go by himself. He stopped by the front counter and informed Linda. He knew his absence would piss off the chief, but Tommy sounded desperate. In addition, he wanted to know more about this woman who had been living in Tito's guesthouse.

Minutes later he sat in his cruiser heading east on Highway 285 to Pojoaque. He drove past the strip of gas stations and fast food joints to the turn-off to Buffalo Thunder, an enormous development, part casino and part Hilton Hotel. He marveled at the number of vehicles in the parking lot. Only mid morning, but already the tourists and gamblers had packed the place.

On his way in he looked for the blue and white Range Rover. He parked as close to the front door as he could, just in case they had to make a quick exit. He avoided the casino part and went directly to the hotel elevator and punched the third floor. When the bell dinged, he walked down the hall quickly to room 352 and knocked. Inside someone shuffled over to the door and looked through the keyhole. "Fernando?" Tommy whispered.

"Yeah, open the door."

Tommy opened the door partway and then undid the chain when he saw his face through the crack.

He brushed past him into the room and stopped dead in his tracks. He found himself face to face with a beautiful young woman with long black hair sitting on the bed. She looked young, criminally young.

Tommy locked the door and then turned quickly to him. "This is Ana. She was living in Tito's guesthouse until recently. I just never had a chance to tell you about her."

"So then she was the person I saw run into the forest." It was not meant as a question.

Tommy nodded. "Let me make a long story short. Ana was one of the young women being held against her will at Three-Hills Ranch. They call it a treatment center, but it's not. It's part of Robert Warner's sex trafficking network. Three-Hills Ranch is a brothel for the filthy rich—old white guys with lots of money. Warner flies them in on his helicopter from L.A. or Vegas. He gets the girls from border towns like Nogales, Agua Prieta, and Juarez. He pays agents there to offer them money and free passage into the country. Once they get to Three-Hills he locks them up and sells them by the hour or by the day, whatever the customer wants."

"How did Tito get involved in this?"

Tommy raised his hand. "Tito was called in to resolve the conflict between A. J. Hoke and Three-Hills. He was horrified when he came to understand what was going on at Three-Hills and threatened to call the sheriff and take the matter to City Council. Warner tried to buy him off by offering him Ana for however long he wanted. You know Tito, he'd always lived alone, but secretly he was a very lonely man. So he agreed, but once he got to know Ana, he regretted what he'd done and decided to take it to the City Council after all. He was afraid to call the sheriff because of his complicity. But he made the fatal mistake of telling Warner about his change of heart. That's why they murdered him."

Now it all made sense to him. Warner's henchmen had carefully chosen the time and place to kill Tito in order to make it look as though it was related to the Entrada dispute. As cover.

"So what's your involvement in all this?"

"None. I mean, I knew about Tito's arrangement because he confided in me. But I wasn't directly involved until Ana showed up at my door after you scared her off from the guesthouse."

He turned to Ana. "Is what he says true?"

She nodded. "Si señor…is all true…can you help us?"

"How many girls are being held at Three-Hills?" he asked.

She shrugged. "It changes…sometimes six, sometimes as many as ten."

"And are they all teenagers?"

Ana nodded.

"From what Ana's told me, they're all between thirteen and eighteen years old," Tommy added. "The majority of them are minors."

He walked to the window and pulled the curtains aside. He placed his hands on the windowsill and looked out at the parking lot, which was getting more crowded by the minute. Didn't anyone work anymore?

Then he turned away from the window and came back to Tommy. "Okay, let's get you out of here. You say two of Warner's men are here following you? How do you know?"

"Because they were watching us downstairs at breakfast. I think they're waiting for us to leave...to get us alone where there isn't a crowd. I didn't know what to do, so I called you."

"All right, then. You come with me, and tell Ana to chain and lock the door after we leave. And tell her not to open the door for anybody except us. Make sure she understands."

Speaking Spanish, Tommy told her what Fernando had said. She nodded her consent.

He opened the door and looked up and down the hallway. All appeared clear. So they stepped outside the door and waited until they heard the click of the lock behind them. He led the way, with Tommy following along behind. They walked the length of the hallway checking all the open rooms, including utility closets and stairways and one room being serviced by housekeeping. They apologized to the startled housekeeper, who looked at them as if she thought they had come to sack the room. Then they took the elevator down to the first floor lobby.

He decided to check the restaurant and bar first, so they walked through the west wing looking for any sign of the two men. Tommy pointed out where they had seen Warner's men at breakfast. Satisfied, they made their way back to the casino and wound their way through the tables and slot machines. Most of the activity at this early hour centered on the slots. The tables were only starting to see action. When they finished in the casino they came back to the lobby. So far they had seen no sign of the two men in khaki.

"Are you sure they're driving a blue and white Range Rover?"

"Yes. I saw the Range Rover in my rear view mirror. They followed us all the way from Santa Fe."

"Let's take a look," he said, passing through automatic doors into the bright sunshine. They walked helter-skelter across the parking lot for a few minutes before he stopped abruptly.

"Wait, let's use our brains. Where would you park if you wanted to remain unnoticed? Certainly not out front here where everyone could see you, right?"

"Probably by a side door or around back."

"Exactly."

He led the way as they circled around to the eastern side of the hotel. Several large vehicles crowded the few parking spaces in front of the side door, including a tour bus from Missouri and a couple of small RVs. No Range Rover, though. So they walked around behind the building and found their view blocked by a one-story laundry building. Carts overflowing with dirty laundry blocked the sidewalk, waiting to be processed. They made their way around the carts and through the tight passageway between the two buildings.

"There it is!" Tommy pointed to a Range Rover parked in front of a service door.

The man inside the Range Rover seemed to be watching them.

He grabbed Tommy and pulled him back into the shadows of the dark passageway. They watched as the man sitting in the driver's seat turned his head away from them and looked straight ahead, as if pretending he hadn't noticed them. Then he sat as still as a statue with his hands seemingly frozen on the steering wheel. One man. Alone. Waiting in the car.

He and Tommy turned to one another.

"Where's the other guy?" both of them said at once.

17

They raced around the building to the side door, with Tommy out front and him trying to catch up. They took the stairway instead of the elevator, bounding up the steps two at a time. On the third floor they stopped to make sure the hallway was clear and then went directly to room 352. He readied his service revolver while Tommy swiped the lock with his keycard.

They entered cautiously, with Tommy stepping back now. The room appeared to be empty, with no sign of Ana. Then they heard a loud groan and the sound of feet shuffling across a tile floor. The bathroom door opened and out walked a weeping Ana, with a man holding her in a one-arm chokehold from behind. He held a pistol in his right hand pressed firmly against her cheek while easing her forward toward the open door to the hallway.

He sized up the stranger coming toward him: tall, gangly, not very muscular, with dirty blond hair and freckles that stood out like pox on his pale skin. Like the others, he wore khaki from head to foot.

What troubled him most was the silencer on the pistol. He could shoot them all and no one would be the wiser. No one would know until housekeeping entered the room.

"Drop your gun," the man said. "Now!"

He did as he was ordered. "Take it easy, friend. Robert Warner wouldn't be happy if you murdered a cop. And neither would you. That's lifetime with no possibility of parole."

"Stand back and no one will get hurt," the man said, all the while easing Ana forward toward the door.

"Think about what you're doing. She's underage. Kidnapping a minor is a federal offense. So is trafficking a minor. If you let her go, you can walk out of here a free man. So put the gun down and let her go. I give you my word that we will let you walk out of here a free man."

"I told you, get out of my way."

The gunman continued to jostle the girl forward awkwardly, one tiny step at a time.

He moved to the side, still trying to convince the gunman to put away his weapon. "Go easy on yourself. You can walk out of here a free man. We won't follow you, I give you my word."

"Back away!" the man shouted.

Then, pushing Ana from behind, the gunman stumbled slightly on the carpet. His arm came loose around her neck for just a split second. Taking advantage of the slack, Ana turned her head quickly and sank her teeth savagely into his arm and then jerked her head side to side like a ravenous beast ripping at his flesh. The man screamed out in pain.

"You little bitch!" he shouted, and threw her to the floor, still holding the pistol in his right hand.

In that split second he chopped his left fist down hard on the man's outreached arm, knocking the pistol free. He kicked the gun to the back of the room and hit him in the stomach with a straight right.

The gunman buckled, groaning. A moment later he came roaring up to grab him around the neck and push him backwards. The two men crashed against the door jam, pinning him momentarily. He tried to kick the gunman in the groin in order to free himself from the chokehold. When he did, the man moved closer so that he didn't have enough space to bring up his knee. The man's hands tightened around his throat, cutting off his oxygen. He felt himself slowly losing consciousness. His vision began to blur, fading to black.

He didn't recognize the sound: zip...zip..zip. The next thing he knew the gunman's hands loosened around his neck and then fell away altogether. He watched as the man's legs buckled and he pitched forward into the open doorway and landed on his face. Bam!

Now directly in front of him stood Ana holding the gun with the silencer. She was crying and talking to someone, maybe him.

When he turned around he saw the man lying on his stomach

in the doorway. Red spots bubbled up on his back and poured onto the carpet. Then he realized what had happened. Ana had shot the gunman. They were all safe. For the moment.

And Tommy? He saw him out in the hallway hiding. Big help Tommy had been.

He walked over and took the gun from Ana's hand. Still weeping, she hugged him tight and sobbed on his shoulder.

"It's okay now, you're safe. He won't hurt you."

"I no want to go back."

"You don't have to go back."

Out in the hallway Tommy was looking over the dead body, still cowering. He seemed afraid to come back inside the room. He stepped outside, took him by the hand, and led him back into the room.

Then he checked the gunman for a pulse. He felt a faint pulse getting fainter by the second. He would be dead in a few minutes, well before an ambulance could get here.

Back inside the room, he took Tommy and Ana over to the bed. "Sit down, both of you."

They did as they were told.

"Here's what's going to happen now. In a few minutes I'm going to call the sheriff and report the shooting. We're fortunate this happened in Santa Fe County, where we work closely with the sheriff's office. The shooting was self-defense, there's no question about that. So I want you to tell them exactly what transpired. Just tell the truth."

He turned to Ana. "Ana, tell them you're here visiting Tommy in Santa Fe. You're his girlfriend, and the two of you are planning to marry. If they ask you how old you are, say you're eighteen. Santa Fe is a sanctuary city, so they won't turn you over to ICE."

"I am eighteen. I mean, for real."

He looked at Tommy, who nodded.

"Good," he said. "Tommy, you tell them the same thing, that the two of your are planning to marry. If they ask, and they probably will, Ana's papers are back at your place in Santa Fe."

He took a step back so he could look at both of them together. "After they finish with their questions, I want you to follow me to Tommy's place. Don't be afraid to go back home. I'll have a cop at your doorstep twenty-four seven until this is all over. We should have a search warrant to enter the ranch today. We'll deal with Warner and his goons when we get there. This should all be over soon. In the meantime I can protect you. If you stay in Santa Fe, that is. Do you understand? Don't try to run again, okay? If you run, I can't help you."

Tommy nodded.

Only then did he call Jodie's cell and briefly explain the situation, telling her what had happened and where they were.

"What? You have one of Warner's girls with you there?"

"I do, and she's given me most of the information we need. She'll testify against Warner."

Jodie was ecstatic. "Hallelujah! This is the break we've been waiting for. I'll be there shortly."

As he finished the call, a young couple came down the hallway and stopped to gawk at the body on the floor. "Is that really blood? Is he dead?" the young woman asked, giggling.

"Move along." He motioned for them to take a hike.

The young woman, a blonde wearing a mini skirt and halter top, giggled again. "You're no fun."

Her boyfriend, a stocky young man with tattoos covering both arms and his neck and wearing a red MAGA cap whisked her away before he could give her a piece of his mind.

He checked the time. He had a good thirty minutes before Jodie arrived. Time enough to take care of the one remaining piece of business. He told Ana and Tommy to stay in the room and lock the door as soon as he left. He started to hand the kidnaper's gun to Tommy but changed his mind and gave it to Ana instead. Then he headed back outside to check on the second man in the Range Rover. Ana wouldn't be safe as long as he was here.

He took the stairway again. Around back he saw the passageway between the two buildings jammed with even more laundry carts, some of them with laundry spilling over their sides onto the pavement. He crept down to the laundry, careful not to make any noise. Then he squeezed between the first couple of carts, stepping on dirty towels and bed sheets that caught at his shoes. Just as he came to the far side of the building he glimpsed a flash of movement out of the corner of his eye.

A laundry cart came hurtling around the side of the building and smashed into him. The blow caught him off guard and knocked him sideways onto a pile of dirty laundry. The cart tipped over and spilled its contents on top of him, leaving him fighting his way out of layers of dirty laundry.

When he surfaced, he came face to face with a thin man dressed in khaki and a blurred object that he recognized too late as the man's fist. The punch clipped him on his left ear and sent him plunging back into the laundry. He lay still for a second to get his bearings and then lunged at the man's waist, knocking him backwards into the wall of the laundry building. They wrestled on the ground, cursing and punching until he ended up on top.

While he reached for his handcuffs, the man in khaki managed to wrestle his right arm free and smacked him in the face with a straight right hand that sent him reeling backwards.

By the time he regained his balance, the stranger had run down to his Range Rover, still parked at the rear entrance to the hotel. The man jumped into the SUV and hit the ignition. He backed up fast, smashing into an empty laundry cart and then into a row of dumpsters.

He limped into the parking lot intent on stopping the man using whatever means necessary.

That changed when he heard tires squealing on the pavement and looked up just in time to see the Range Rover coming directly at him. Instinctively he dived to his left and rolled on the hard pavement as the Range Rover roared past in a burst of wind. A split second later and he would have been splattered all over the pavement.

He sat up, taking stock of his situation. His knuckles were raw and his back ached from the fall, but otherwise he seemed intact. He got to his feet slowly and looked around for the Range Rover. He spotted it at the end of the Buffalo Thunder driveway turning left onto the highway. It headed East toward Santa Fe, presumably on its way back to Galisteo.

He watched the Range Rover disappear in traffic and then returned to the hotel. Back in the room he found Tommy and Ana still sitting on the bed, waiting for the sheriff. None of them spoke.

Fifteen minutes later Jodie and another deputy arrived, with an ambulance waiting outside. He again explained the situation, this time in more detail. The deputies took notes and jotted down contact information, and then Jodie took Ana aside and asked her questions about Warner and Three-Hills Ranch for over an hour. When she finished, she said they could leave. She and her deputy would wait until forensics finished and the body had been transported to the morgue, however long it took.

On his way out Jodie grabbed him by the arm and said, "We're in! Ana's testimony will get us a search warrant. I didn't give you enough credit!"

He took that as a high compliment.

18

While Tommy checked out of the hotel, Ana packed her clothes and gathered their belongings. Then she followed him to the lobby of Buffalo Thunder to meet Tommy. Outside, they walked together to Tommy's Subaru. He insisted they follow him back to Santa Fe, just in case the man in the Range Rover reappeared. So while they waited he brought his cruiser around to their Subaru and then led the way out to the highway.

Coming up the long hill to the Santa Fe Opera he thought he spotted a white and blue Range Rover following Tommy's Subaru in his rear view mirror. When he slowed down to a sluggish fifty mph, both the Subaru and Range Rover did too. In response, he flicked his turn signal on and off several times for Tommy to see. He waited until the last second and then turned sharply onto the Tesuque exit, with Tommy following closely behind. The Range Rover seemed to have disappeared when he checked his mirror again.

Relieved, he drove through Tesuque and took Bishop's Lodge Road into Santa Fe. At the Scottish Rites Masonic Temple they turned left onto the Paseo and followed it around to Don Gaspar and up the street to Tommy's apartment, across from a small park. While Tommy and Ana waited outside, he went into the apartment to check for unwanted guests. He found nothing amiss and no intruders. Even so, he waited until they were safely in the house with all the doors and windows locked tight before leaving. On his way out he promised to send them protection as soon as he got to the station and cleared it with the chief.

"Do you have a weapon?"

"You mean a gun? No," Tommy said.

"Well, then keep your doors locked. I should have someone here in less than an hour."

After making sure the door was locked behind him, he walked to his cruiser and headed downtown to Washington Avenue.

Linda stopped him as he walked into the station. "Fernando, I have a message for you. A woman called this morning. Let's see if I can find it," she said, searching for the message on the cluttered counter. "Here it is. From a Mrs. Esther Hoke. She called earlier to file a missing persons report. It seems her husband has been missing since last night. She wanted me to tell you personally. She wouldn't talk to anyone else."

The news rattled him. Too much was happening all at once. He would have to ask Antonio for help.

Back in his office he checked his voice messages. The first was from Estelle wanting him to stop at Kaune's Market on his way home for groceries. She gave him a list of what she needed. The second was from Ruben wanting to know what he intended to do about Henry and his Pueblo followers taking over the Palace of the Governors. The third was from Jodie saying she would try to call back later today.

As soon as he finished listening to the messages, he went down the hall to Chief Stuart's office. He started by apologizing for missing their morning briefing, which seemed to ease the tension between them. Then he provided a full account of his morning's activities and asked that protection be assigned for Tommy Baca and Ana. The chief agreed to send someone over immediately.

Back in his office he sat at his desk staring at the window across the room. A sort of paralysis had overtaken him. He had no idea what to do next. So he called Antonio and asked if he wanted to go to the Shed for a late lunch.

"Your treat?" Antonio asked.

"Of course."

Antonio never refused an opportunity to eat at the Shed as long as someone else picked up the check. Over the Shed's famous red chile chicken enchiladas and mocha cake, he brought Antonio up to speed on Tommy and the morning's developments.

He'd just returned to his office when his phone rang. "Fernando, this is Jodie Williams. I have bad news. Something stinks to high heaven here. Judge Richardson again refused our request for a search warrant, even with this new evidence. What do you know about this guy?"

"Not a lot. I know he's given the D.A. a hard time on some prosecutions. He's kind of arrogant. Not all that friendly."

"Yeah, well I've done some research. He's from the East Coast, not from around here. He went to Yale Law School and somehow ended up in Santa Fe. He lives at Tano Falls, the most exclusive country club subdivision in the city. In other words, he's rich and well connected."

"Does he know Robert Warner?"

"You tell me! Something is rotten here, that's all I know. We've presented him with more than enough evidence for a search warrant."

He didn't know what to say.

"I'm going to keep trying. We're taking our case to another judge later today. I'll let you know if anything breaks."

The line went dead.

19

On their way to visit Esther Hoke he and Antonio had time to discuss what they knew about Warner and the alleged illegal trafficking at Three-Hills Ranch, including the information Ana had provided. Antonio wanted to bust Warner immediately, but he cautioned against it.

"We don't know. Ana might not be reliable. Or she might not stand up to Warner's lawyers in court. We need additional witnesses who'll corroborate what she says. I'm sure Warner has the best lawyers money can buy."

"More hired guns," Antonio added as they crossed the bridge over the Galisteo River.

Once past the bridge they sailed around the long curve and pulled into the driveway to the Hoke Ranch. The driveway took them directly to the little house with the porch. This time the two border collies met them at the house, barking as before. Antonio jumped out first, needing to stretch his long legs. At six feet seven he could never get comfortable in a cruiser, no matter how far back he moved the seat. He climbed out and greeted the border collies. The dogs sniffed him a few times and then returned to the shade of the porch.

Antonio followed him up the steps to the porch and waited while he knocked on the door.

"Who is it?" a woman's voice shouted from inside the house. She sounded angry and suspicious of who might be knocking on her door.

He realized he should have telephoned first. He should have called to let her know he was coming and bringing company.

"Go away or I'll shoot!"

He stepped off the porch and looked around. He went to a side window and looked in through a thin curtain. Esther Hoke sat in a cane-back chair in the hallway facing the front door. In her lap she held a double barrel shotgun pointed directly at the door.

He walked back to the door. "Mrs. Hoke, it's Detective Fernando Lopez from the Santa Fe Police Department. I got your message about your husband missing. Can we talk?"

Silence. Then the door opened an inch or two. Her right eye appeared in the opening. "Detective Lopez! Come on in! I'm so sorry. You didn't call back, so I wasn't expecting you."

"It's my fault, I should have called."

They walked into a dark, dusty room with closed windows and drawn curtains. The temperature in the house must have been close to ninety degrees. She led them back to a kitchen with a linoleum floor and unpainted cabinets. Along one wall stood a wood burning stove, complete with an array of cast iron skillets on top and hanging from the ceiling.

She stood her shotgun in one corner of the room and motioned for them to sit down at the kitchen table. As they sat down, he introduced Antonio.

"Pleased to meet you. I'd offer you a cold drink but I haven't anything made today. I'm all flustered since A. J. disappeared. To tell you the truth, I'm scared to death."

"What are you afraid of?" he asked, noticing how ancient the woman looked up close. Her translucent skin and watery gray eyes, combined with her long white ponytail, gave her an ethereal quality he'd seen only in the very old. Or the very dead.

"I'm afraid of those hoodlums and perverts next door, that's who I'm afraid of. The last thing A. J. told me before he left was to lock the door and don't answer it under any circumstances whatsoever. So I got out my old four ten shotgun just in case they show up here. I haven't shot it in years, but I used to be a pretty darn good shot, believe you me."

"So then A. J. hasn't returned."

She shook her head solemnly.

"Do you know where he was going?"

She looked down at her hands, which were shaking on the table now. "He was going over there to settle things."

Tears appeared in her eyes as she spoke. "I told him not to go, but he wouldn't listen. You know how men are—they're so darned stubborn, especially old men. I'm so afraid something bad has happened to him."

"What did he mean by 'settle things'?"

She wiped her eyes with the back of her hand.

"I'm sorry, I know this is a difficult time. But I need to ask you a few more questions. Did he take a gun with him?"

She nodded. "He took his twelve gauge."

Antonio sighed.

"What time did he leave last night?"

"Late afternoon. About five, I think."

"Did he drive? Did he take the Chevy pickup I saw out in the yard the last time I was here?"

"Yes sir. He loves that old truck."

"And you've heard nothing from him since he left."

She shook her head, the tears sliding down her pale cheeks.

"Well...," he said, looking at Antonio. "We'll find your husband, Mrs. Hoke. It may take a while, but we'll find him. I promise you that."

She took a handkerchief out of her skirt pocket and wiped her eyes.

"But these people are dangerous. I wish he hadn't gone over there by himself."

"Me too. Did he tell you what they did to that young girl who ran away and came over here for help?" she asked.

"He did."

"They beat that poor child almost to death. Right there on our front porch. I didn't tell A. J., but I took a video of the whole thing with my cell phone. Took it from the front window."

"Really? Can I see the video?"

"I don't see why not."

She went into a back bedroom and returned with her cell phone. She handed the phone to him.

He clicked the play arrow and then watched in disgust as the man who called himself the Foreman beat the scantily clad girl mercilessly. The girl screamed and begged him to stop as he smacked her around the porch with the back of his hand. He had to look closely at the long dark hair, but he thought he recognized Ana in the fuzzy video. Or someone who looked like Ana.

"The man who did this deserves to be horse-whipped."

"Or worse," Antonio replied. "I'd like to have him alone for about ten minutes. That's all it would take."

"We need this for evidence. Can you send it to me by email?" He handed back her phone.

"I guess...but how do I do it?"

"Here, let me show you."

He took the phone from her hand and then hit the email share button on her phone. Then he typed in his email address at the station and hit send. The phone dinged success.

He looked around. "I'm not sure it's safe for you to stay here alone. Would you like to come to Santa Fe for a few days, just until we find your husband? We could put you up in a safe house where you wouldn't have to worry about your neighbors."

"No, I can't leave the ranch. Not without knowing what's happened to A. J. Plus I have chores to attend. I can't just pick up and walk away."

"Do you have transportation? Can you get to town for supplies and the things you need?"

She nodded. "Oh sure, my Ford is parked in the garage. I can take care of myself. And we have a son who lives down in Socorro. I'll give him a call if I need something."

"Okay, but if you change your mind, call me and we'll come right out. I'm serious."

He wrote down his cell phone number on the back of his card and handed it to her.

"I will. I promise." She gave them a half-hearted smile as they all stood up from the table.

"Do you mind if we look around the ranch a bit?"

"No, help yourself," she said.

With that, she showed them to the front door. They heard her latch the door behind them.

He followed Antonio down the porch steps into the late afternoon light. Sunset wasn't far off. Somehow he'd totally lost track of time. It had been that kind of day. And it wasn't over yet.

Antonio waited for him by the cruiser. "So now you have a green light. You don't have to wait."

"What do you mean?"

"You don't need to wait for a search warrant. You have a missing person report and you know damn well where that missing person went. Let's drive right in and confront the motherfuckers."

"No, we'll wait for the search warrant," he said. "It has to be done in daylight…and I know one other person who wants a piece of these pervs. She'll want to come along too."

Antonio mumbled something that he didn't catch.

"Let's drive around the ranch and take a look." He climbed into the cruiser. Antonio did the same, still grumbling.

He drove through the yard, past an open barn, and around a corral where a small herd of cattle lolled about staring at the cruiser. Beyond the corral the dirt road became a thin ribbon, with tire tracks extending across the smoky mesa to the hills beyond. Touches of Fall color brightened the normally muted landscape, highlighted now by banks of purple sage and yellow blooming chamisa. Their enjoyment of the September colors ended abruptly when Antonio spotted something troubling up ahead: a brown object on the ground surrounded by black and red flecked vultures.

"Wait, what's that?"

He slowed to a stop about twenty yards away. They smelled the dead carcass even before they opened their car doors. The vultures scattered as they climbed out of the cruiser and approached the badly decomposed remains of a cow. He covered his mouth and nose with a handkerchief and crept closer, noticing the gaping bullet holes in the side of the cow. Hadn't Hoke told him that Warner's men used his cows for target practice? The spectacle disgusted him. He waved at Antonio to stay back and returned to the cruiser.

They found two more carcasses as they followed the tire tracks across the mesa, not bothering to stop. Finally they came to a barbed wire fence with a bleached white steer's skull atop one of the fence posts. The steer watched them approach with empty eye sockets. When they stepped out of the cruiser, they noticed that many of the fence posts had similar skulls attached, as if they were intended as a macabre warning to potential invaders from Warner's ranch. They had come to the northern boundary of the Hoke property.

From the fence they could see the Galisteo River below, with the road into Warner's ranch on the far side of the river. Even more interesting, Hoke's rusted pickup had been left parked on Hoke's side of the riverbank.

"Let's check it out," he said.

They took turns spreading the barbed wire strands for each other and stepping through the fence. Then they walked down a rocky slope to the pickup, its bed empty except for a shovel and two bales of hay. Hoke hadn't bothered to lock the cabin door. Inside they saw an open box of twelve gauge shotgun shells on the seat. On examination they found three shells missing from the box.

He and Antonio looked at each other.

"Not good," Antonio said.

20
FRIDAY

Morning sunshine struck the bullet holes at just the right angle to make them glow like pencil points of light. During the night someone had sprayed the front of the Palace of the Governors with automatic weapon fire that left nicks in the stucco siding and what looked like drill holes in the heavy wooden door. He and Manny stood alongside Chief Stuart examining a cardboard proclamation posted on the door. The crude handwriting read: "Get the Indans out by five this afternoon or they will be drove out at gunpoint."

As an exclamation point of sorts, the writer had attached the cardboard epistle to the door by means of a twelve-inch Bowie knife sunk a full inch into the wooden door.

"Not exactly Luther's ninety-five theses," said Manny, always a wise ass. "Whoever wrote it can't spell Indians. Plus he confuses the past tense for the past participle of drive."

Chief Stuart gave Manny a dirty look. He scowled at the handwritten edict, black magic marker on an 81/2 x 11 sheet of gray cardboard.

"Do you think this is Ruben Ortega's work?"

"Hard to imagine Ruben being this reckless. Not with guns. That's not the way he works."

The chief looked skeptical. "I want you to talk to Ortega today. Do whatever it takes to make peace. Promise him anything. We'll worry about Henry Ortiz later. We can't have people shooting each other on the Plaza."

"Will do."

"And Fernando, get forensics over here to bag the evidence before it disappears. I don't want some idiot to pick it up as a souvenir."

With that, Chief Stuart walked off with one last frown at Manny, who gave him a mock salute.

They waited until the chief was out of hearing range before they spoke. "What's wrong with you? One of these days you're going to really piss him off," he said.

"Hah! You're a fine one to talk. You're barely on speaking terms with the chief."

"That's different. I have my reasons. You're just being a wise ass."

Manny lowered his head. "I know. Sometimes I just can't help myself. He's so uptight."

"Be careful, that's all I'm saying."

"I hear you."

He looked up and down Palace Avenue. "Okay, so why don't you take care of forensics, and I'll deal with Ruben. I'm going back to my office to call him right now. If he doesn't answer his phone, I'll drive out to Apache Canyon."

When he turned to go, he saw homeless Bill sitting across the street on the curb watching him. Bill often panhandled on the Plaza, but usually later in the day, not at this early hour of the morning. Bill motioned toward his eyes with two fingers and then waved him over.

"It's a little early for you, isn't it, Bill?" he said, walking over to the curb as requested.

"Nah, I slept in the doorway of the Plaza Café last night. Never made it back to camp."

"Why's that?"

"Me and Eddie had a few drinks, that's why. I don't know what the hell happened to Eddie. You guys probably threw him in the drunk tank. Wouldn't be the first time."

"Eddie's the guy I saw in your camp the other day? The skinny guy?"

Bill nodded. "The one and only."

"So what do you want?"

Bill pointed to his eyes. "Like I told you before, I see everything around town. I saw who shot up the Palace last night. If you refresh my memory, I just might tell you who did it."

He looked at Bill skeptically. "I'll give you five dollars, not a penny more."

"Getting cheap, are you?" Bill asked. "Well, it's too early in the morning to haggle, I suppose. Plus I'm hungry. So you got yourself a deal." He held out his hand.

He deposited a five note in Bill's hand.

"So here's what happened. Early this morning two teenagers came roaring down Palace Avenue on one of those miniature motorcycles, whatever they're called."

"You mean a scooter, like a Vespa?"

"Yeah, one of them. Anyway, they stopped right in front of the Palace and the teenager on the back jumped off. He ran up to the door and stuck up that cardboard notice with a big knife. Then he ran back to the scooter and sprayed the building with bullets. Sounded like some sort of automatic weapon. The two of them drove off as fast as they came, made a helluva noise."

"Did you see a license plate, anything that would identify them?"

Bill laughed. "Hell no, I was half asleep. Plus I can't see for shit when it comes to distances."

"But you did see the scooter and the two teenagers?"

"Yeah! I can see that good, just not the small stuff like license plates."

"Anything else you can remember?"

"Nope. That just about drains my memory."

On his way to the station he considered what Bill had told him. Old Bill couldn't be considered a reliable witness by any stretch of the imagination. Still, if the basics of his story were true, then Ruben and his posse had nothing to do with the shooting. He hoped that was the case.

He turned the corner onto Washington Avenue, walking away from the nearly deserted Plaza. At the end of a week Fiesta had just about run its course. The food and beverage tents still remained, but the party animals had stayed home, tired, cranky, hung-over, or otherwise indisposed after a weeklong binge of festivities. The few events remaining over the weekend would draw only a smattering of diehards before Fiesta ended with a whimper on Monday.

Back in his office he dialed Ruben's number and let it ring when there was no answer. When the recording came on, he said, "Ruben, this is Fernando. We need to talk. I have a proposition for you that I hope will end this standoff. I don't know if you're involved in the threat to attack the Palace this evening, but I hope not. If you are, call off your troops. Otherwise everyone's going to end up in jail. Or worse. Call me back!"

He debated whether to wait a few minutes and call again or to drive out to Ruben's ranch in Apache Canyon. Maybe Ruben wasn't answering his phone because of all the turmoil. Before he could reach a decision his phone rang.

"Ruben?" he said, expecting the callback.

"No, it's Jodie Williams, Fernando," the voice said. "Good news. Judge Hernandez has approved the search warrant. We took it to him after we realized Richardson wasn't going to act. For whatever reason."

"Okay, so when are you planning to do this? I'm caught up in this Plaza standoff today."

There was silence on the other end. "Well, when can you get free? We really need your help. We're shorthanded over here, critically shorthanded. We're counting on you."

He considered, finding it difficult to say no to her. "How soon can you get started?"

"I can leave right now and bring John Rodriguez with me. It shouldn't take us more than a couple of hours. You could still be back by noon or shortly thereafter."

He agreed, reluctantly. It would be another crazy day.

He had no trouble recruiting Antonio, who was eager to confront Warner. "Hell yes!" the big man said.

Then he informed Linda about where he was going, promising to be back by mid-afternoon to deal with Ruben and the Caballeros and whoever else was shooting up the Plaza.

"Make sure you are, Fernando," he heard Linda say behind him as he bolted out the door.

21

On their way to Three-Hills Ranch Antonio chatted nonstop. He seemed especially cheerful, looking forward to the confrontation that awaited them. Him, not so much. He worried they should have brought more manpower. He worried about Warner and his gunmen and what they were capable of doing. He worried about everything that could go wrong.

Shortly before ten they found themselves approaching the intersection of highways 285 and 41 in their cruiser. As before, Jodie was waiting roadside with her companion, John Rodriguez. He pulled in beside her cruiser and lowered his window.

"You lead the way, we'll follow," she said from her open window. "And go in fast. Let them know we mean business."

So he led the way, taking them down Highway 41 to the bridge over the Galisteo River. Approaching the bridge, he slowed just enough to bounce over the lip of the riverbank and get traction in the sandy riverbed.

Jodie followed closely behind, urging him to go even faster.

At the turn-off to the ranch they saw Hoke's rusted Chevy pickup still parked on the opposite site of the river. When they cleared the bank onto the gravel road into Three-Hills Ranch, he hit the gas pedal and roared though the rock formations at the entrance. The two cars passed by the guardhouse in a cloud of dust and came to an abrupt stop halfway between the compound and the barracks. They waited in their cruisers until the dust settled.

Out of his rear view mirror he saw the Foreman leave the guardhouse and hurry over to meet them. He and Antonio jumped out of their cruiser first, and then Jodie and John did the same.

The Foreman paused. "This is private property."

"And this is a search warrant." Jodie showed him the document. "Now stand back and get out of the way, sir."

Not happy, the Foreman stepped back and glanced up at the helipad on the hill above the house, where Warner's Sikorsky rested. Then he turned and glared at the four of them.

Antonio made a point of walking right up to and past the Foreman. The Foreman was a big man with lots of muscles, but at 6'7" and 280 pounds, Antonio was in a different class entirely. He intimidated everyone.

Jodie led the way, heading for the barracks. The rest of them followed her. They climbed the steps to the porch and then marched into the elongated wooden building. They found a dormitory style interior divided by half-walls into ten bedrooms or living units, each with a bed, bureau, and sitting chair. A common bathroom containing sinks, showers, and toilet stalls occupied the opposite end of the long room. The bathroom had no doors, so the only privacy in the dormitory would be in the toilet stalls. Ceiling fans hung from the exposed rafters overhead, stirring the hot, stuffy air.

The cubicles appeared deserted, with not even a stick of clothing or a toiletry item indicating the recent presence of young women. Instead, they found themselves face to face with an older woman wearing a white jacket with her arms folded across her chest. A tall thin blonde, her nametag identified her as Joan Novak. She appeared to be expecting them.

"Can I help you?" she asked firmly.

"You can stand aside. We have a warrant to search the property." Jodie showed her the search warrant.

"Can I help you find what you're looking for?"

"We're looking for the young women who were here earlier this week," he said. "What happened to them? And who are you?"

"I'm the unit psychiatrist, Joan Novak. And as for the young women, they've all been discharged and sent home."

"All of them? At the same time?"

"Not exactly at the same time, but you have to understand that we run an expedited, two-week detox program here. We find a short, intensive program more effective than the usual four to six weeks."

Jodie looked at her skeptically. "What kind of intensive program?"

"We have a three-step program: acknowledging the problem, treating the addiction, and planning for the future. We employ group and one-on-one therapy as well as medication, of course."

He stepped around Jodie and stood face to face with the woman. "We have direct testimony from one of the women formerly held here that you and Robert Warner are running a sex trafficking ring for wealthy men. Men who Warner flies in on his helicopter."

The woman shook her head. "You must mean Ana. She's not well, I'm afraid. She ran away some time ago. Her parents brought her here after she had a schizophrenic episode probably brought on by heavy drug use. She was hearing voices and having paranoid thoughts about people following her and even trying to kill her. I wouldn't be surprised if she's stopped taking her meds since she ran away. She's just not very responsible."

"What about the two young women who we found murdered on Highway forty-one not far from here?" Jodie shot back. "Did they have schizophrenia too?"

The woman seemed surprised, or pretended to. "I don't know anything about them."

Without responding, Jodie brushed past the woman and walked through the building looking into all the cubicles and then the common bathroom at the end. He and the others followed, leaving Novak standing with her arms folded watching them.

Everything appeared deserted, including the bathroom. Likewise, all the drawers in all the cubicles were empty.

Frustrated, they decided to split up. Jodie went to search the nearby barn, while John headed for the garage and the other smaller outbuildings on the perimeter of the property.

He and Antonio walked over to the mansion, with the Foreman following at a safe distance. The closer they came to the mansion the more massive it appeared: an enormous four-sided structure with patios, terraces, turrets, and multiple banks of windows on every side. Small but elaborate gardens surrounded the house, with benches and gazebos and a water ditch that resembled a moat. In fact, the walkway to the front door passed over the ditch like a drawbridge. It was clearly meant to evoke the feeling of a castle.

He pressed a doorbell that rang a chime inside the house. Momentarily the door opened wide and Warner himself stood before them. He looked like an aging actor, short with chemically dark hair and pancake makeup giving him an artificial tan and covering up deep wrinkles and other facial imperfections. White slacks and a navy blue linen shirt added to his casual, relaxed look. He clearly wanted to be seen as an easygoing, breezy kind of guy, not a multi-millionaire pedophile running a sex-trafficking ring.

"Hello. What can I do for you, officers?" he asked cheerfully, his wide smile revealing a mouthful of ultra white teeth.

"We're looking for A. J. Hoke, the neighbor you've been quarreling with. Mr. Hoke came over here two nights ago and hasn't been seen since then."

"Yes, I remember. We had an interesting discussion. He must have gotten lost in the dark on his way home. We really need to add more lighting to make Three-Hills more accessible."

"What time did he leave?"

"Well, it must have been after seven. I remember it was nearly dark when he left."

"Did he drive, or was he on foot?"

"He walked in, if I remember correctly, but he may have parked down by the river, I don't know. Our two properties adjoin, you see. The Galisteo River separates the two."

"What did you two discuss? He had complained about you to Tito Garcia. In fact, he wanted Tito to take his complaint to the Santa Fe City Council. What was that all about?"

Warner's eyes narrowed. "Well, he claimed we were making too much noise, that the noise was frightening his animals. I told him I would make sure the noise did not continue. You see how quiet it is today?" He opened his arms wide, as if showcasing his quiet ranch.

He nodded. "And you haven't seen or heard from him since he left that night?"

Warner shook his head. "No, I've had no contact with him."

Antonio stepped forward, deciding to play bad cop to his good cop. "We're also investigating reports of young girls being held here against their will. Girls who are being trafficked for sex."

Warner winced at the sound of 'girls' but quickly recovered and resumed his sales pitch. "We do hold young women here, some of them against their will, but only to the extent that our patients are sent here by their parents. Three-Hills Treatment Center is a private facility to treat drug and alcohol addiction. A detox center, if you will. We offer an intensive two-week program that has proven highly successful. If you're interested in hearing more about our program, you should speak with our head psychiatrist, Dr. Joan Novak. She can give you more specifics. I'm just the CEO, what do I know?" he said, laughing.

"Then do you mind if we look around?" he asked, ignoring Warner's attempt at humor.

"No, please come in. I'll give you a tour of the house."

They followed Warner through the foyer into an enormous front room that occupied the entire north wing of the house. Even more spectacular, the rear wall of the room was glass through which you could see the courtyard in the center of the house. Through the glass they saw a water fountain surrounded by benches and exotic plantings, everything from saguaro cactus to banana trees.

Warner pointed out the various rooms as they walked down the other three corridors surrounding the interior courtyard. The house included a full gym, media room, and office in addition to the usual kitchen, dining room, and bathrooms. The entire south wing consisted of ten bedrooms, all of them decorated in garish shades of red and purple. The last two had heart-shaped beds, the kind you saw at cheap love motels near the border.

Warner seemed somewhat embarrassed by the love bedrooms. "For romantic getaways," he said by way of explanation.

"Romantic getaways for your clients?" Antonio asked.

Warner cleared his throat. "Well, for our parents...when they bring their daughters here for treatment...it makes their stay sort of special."

Antonio rolled his eyes.

They finished the tour at the foyer where they'd entered. Warner cheerfully wished them well and said he hoped Mr. Hoke turned up soon. "He seemed like a fine fellow."

"By the way, is your helicopter a Sikorsky?" he asked before they left the house.

"Yes, it's their Executive model. I have a pilot on call at the Santa Fe Airport, but I love flying, so I usually fly it myself. I'm a licensed pilot, among other things."

"Do you mind if we take a look at it on our way out."

"No, help yourself. It's a terrific machine!"

Warner quickly closed the door behind them.

As they made their way around the side of the house to the helipad Antonio mumbled to himself. "Among other things! I can imagine!"

The helipad had been carved out of the smallest of the three hills that encircled the bowl in which the ranch was situated. A series of steps took them up to the concrete slab where the blue and white Sikorsky waited, its long rotor blades extending over the sides of the helipad.

He checked out the cockpit while Antonio looked into the cabin, finding nothing amiss. "What are we looking for?" Antonio asked.

He didn't have an answer.

Antonio mumbled to himself, this time about the "filthy rich," as they hiked back down to the yard. The Foreman still stood in the yard watching them. He hadn't moved the entire time.

Jodie and John were waiting for them at the barracks. "Did you talk to Warner?" Jodie asked.

He nodded. "Yeah. He repeated what Joan Novak said. Same, identical script."

"He's a real salesman. Slicker than you know what."

Before leaving, the four of them made plans to meet at the intersection of highways 285 and 41 for a briefing. On their way he and Antonio stopped on the riverbank, across from where Hoke's pickup was parked. They walked to the pickup and looked it over again.

Nothing had changed since last time. The open box of twelve gauge shotgun shells remained untouched on the seat. As before, only three shells were missing from the box.

Finished, they drove back to Highway 41 and up to the intersection with 285. Jodie was standing beside her cruiser when they pulled into the gravel lot. She walked over and waited until he lowered his window. "You're always late."

"Sorry, we wanted to check out Hoke's pickup again." He climbed out of the cruiser to join them.

"Well, we've been busy too. John called back to the station and had them check on Joan Novak. And what do you know, the American Psychiatric Association has no record of a Joan Novak."

He nodded. "Although she could be licensed in another country. She does have sort of an odd accent. I can't place it."

"What, are you saying you believe her?"

"No, but I think we should consider all possibilities. What do you think, John?"

"I think she's bogus. If she were a real psychiatrist she wouldn't be so glib about detox. She wouldn't brag about the success of a two-week intensive program for addicts and alcoholics. It's not realistic."

"And what about the young women?" Antonio asked. "You can't tell me all of them were discharged at the same time. That's bullshit!"

He nodded. "So where are the young women?" The question hung in the air like a bad smell. When no one ventured a response, he continued. "And what happened to Hoke?"

Jodie sighed. "We don't have the staffing or the wherewithal to search two huge ranches, and neither do you. Even if we used a drone, I don't think it would give us enough detail to find an unmarked grave."

None of them disagreed.

"Well, here's the situation. We don't have enough evidence to bring anyone in right now. But there may be one person who can help us out. That's Ana, the young woman who escaped. She's staying with Tommy Baca, who was Tito Garcia's assistant. She may have information about Joan Novak. She may even have an idea about where the other women might have gone. I'll talk with her this afternoon and get back to you. Okay?"

Jodie agreed. "Okay, and in the meantime we'll do more research on this Joan Novak."

"If that's her real name," John added.

22

Linda flagged him down as he walked into the station. "Fernando, Ruben Ortega has been trying to reach you all morning. He's called several times but wouldn't leave a message. He says he needs to talk to you in person. Nobody else, just you."

"Okay, thanks."

He called Ruben from his office as soon as he sat down. This time he answered immediately.

"Where have you been, Lopez? I've been calling all day. We need to talk right away about the Palace of the Governors situation. I want you to know that I had nothing to do with this bullshit. Bunch of young hotheads put up that note. They're the ones threatening to show up with guns this afternoon. None of my people are involved, I swear to God. Are you listening?"

"I hear you, Ruben."

"I'm worried that we'll be blamed, or worse yet the Caballeros will be blamed, even though none of my posse or the Caballeros would ever do anything this stupid. It's this new group of young hotheads, like I said. They think violence is the only solution—that they can take what they want by force. Are you listening? Why don't you say something?"

"Because I can't get a word in edgewise, that's why. What do you think?"

"Can you meet me downtown in thirty minutes?"

"Sure. Where?"

"I'll be at the La Fonda bar in thirty!" he said and hung up.

He waited about twenty minutes before walking over to La Fonda. He saw a few more people on the street than he'd seen that morning, but nothing like the crowds earlier in the week at the beginning of Fiesta. Chief Stuart had wisely positioned a small group of Santa Fe's finest in front of the Palace of the Governors, just in case trouble started. A couple of Native American vendors had shown up to sell their jewelry under the portico, while inside Henry and his followers still occupied the museum with the front doors barricaded.

Ruben and his right-hand man Larry Aragon were waiting for him in the bar when he stepped inside La Fonda. Ruben waved at him from a small table against the back wall.

He walked across the lobby and joined them at their table. Both Ruben and Larry were drinking beers. He ordered the same.

Ruben looked at him. "I didn't know you guys could drink while on duty."

"We can't. This is my lunch break." He raised his Modelo Especial.

"Like I said—"

He raised his hand, cutting Ruben off. "First, let me tell you something you need to know. Tito wasn't killed because of the cancellation of the Entrada. The Entrada had nothing whatsoever to do with his death. He was murdered by rich people trafficking young girls for sex at a ranch south of the city. Tito found out about this and was planning to take the issue to City Council at their meeting next week. The traffickers timed the killing so that we would think it was related to the ongoing feud over the Entrada. Do you understand what I'm saying? The time and place of the killing was meant to distract us from the real reason. It was a hoax. A red herring."

Ruben listened closely without responding.

"The fact of the matter is that the vast majority of Santa Fe agrees that we should cancel the Entrada for the common good—not only to keep the peace, but to promote conciliation and cooperation between the different cultures. Especially today when our national politics is so fractured, people here want to celebrate what brings us together, not what divides us."

Ruben continued to drink his beer in silence.

He paused a moment to give Ruben time to digest everything he'd just said. "So here's my proposal. Henry Ortiz and his followers will end their occupation of the Palace and agree to never occupy it again...if you and the Caballeros will agree to abide by the deal to permanently cancel the Entrada. He's willing to work with you to celebrate the long tradition of Hispanic/Native American cooperation in the city. Two cultures, one very special city."

"You're forgetting the Anglos."

"Okay, three cultures. That's what makes Santa Fe special."

Ruben sighed. "Yeah, I've heard all this before. It's true, but it's still hard for some of us to lose our traditions in the name of peace or political correctness or whatever you want to call it. But I'll talk to my guys anyway. I suppose we can make the Entrada a private event somewhere on private property, instead of a public re-enactment. That is, as long as we aren't asked to give up more of our traditions. Understand? No more takeaways."

"Of course. I feel the same way. Absolutely."

Larry set his beer on the table. "That's fine, the agreement you're offering. But you know what? It's downright annoying that no one asks the Pueblos to give up celebrating their rebellion. All we hear about is how divisive the Entrada is, but how about the sixteen eighty Pueblo Revolt? That's not divisive? Why doesn't the city go after them?"

"Well, whatever they do to celebrate sixteen eighty, they do privately. It's not part of the Fiesta."

Larry took another drink of his beer and wiped the foam from his moustache. "I suppose, but we always read in the *Independent* about the heroes of sixteen eighty, while De Vargas and the Caballeros are presented in the media and by all these so-called reconciliation groups as mass murderers. Why can't we celebrate the founding of Santa Fe in sixteen ten or its reunification in sixteen ninety-two? Do you hear what I'm saying?"

"I like that. The reunification. It works for me."

Ruben waved his arms. "Okay, enough. We could argue about this all day, but we don't have the time."

Ruben turned to him. "So you need to take this peace offering to Henry Ortiz and get him out of the Palace before the hotheads arrive. I can't stop these punks if they show up at five o'clock with guns. I have no control over them, none. Nobody does as far as I know."

"So who are these guys?"

"They call themselves the Cavalier Club. I guess they picture themselves as knights or something like that. They have nothing to do with the Caballeros."

"Hah! That's funny!" Larry said. "They're just a bunch of young pisants who like to cause trouble."

He raised his hand. "Yeah, but they have guns. You say you have no control over them, but I still think your presence would help keep the peace if Henry comes out of the Palace and the two of you shake hands in public. Can you stick around at least long enough to do that?"

Ruben considered for a moment. "Okay, I'll do it for Tito. It'll be my way of honoring him."

They finished their beers and headed for the Plaza.

23

The action had already started when the three of them crossed San Francisco Street onto the Plaza. Several young men carrying an assortment of weapons had gathered on the bandstand across the street from the Palace of the Governors. One of them held a megaphone in one hand and what looked like an AR-15 in the other. The kid looked young enough to be in high school. Across the street Antonio and eight other officers were staring down the hotheads. He knew the chief had their SWAT team on standby at the station. If any shots were fired, all hell would break loose.

Ruben pointed to the bandstand. "Now you see what I mean. Look at them, just a bunch of teenagers."

"The kid with the AR-fifteen looks like he's sixteen years old," he replied, shocked at the sight of the skinny kid wearing fatigues with his long black hair slicked back.

"That's Ricky Lucero, he's dangerous. He called my boys pussies because we wouldn't take back the Palace by force. He's just showing off to his friends to prove he's a tough guy."

"He's a piece of work," Larry added. "He calls his followers a club, but what he's really trying to do is form his own militia. As someone who served in Iraq, I take offense at that. Big time."

He agreed. "Yeah, and we can't do a damn thing about it, thanks to the wisdom of our state legislators who passed an open carry law. People who carry guns have to actually threaten someone before we can take away their weapons. By that time it's usually too late."

Antonio spotted them talking and walked across the Plaza to join them. "Who are these punks?"

"They aren't members of the Caballeros, that's for damned sure," Ruben said. "They call themselves the Cavalier Club, a bunch of young lowlifes who like to cause trouble."

As the four of them walked by the bandstand Antonio paused for a few seconds to give Ricky Lucero the evil eye. In response, Lucero raised his megaphone and shouted: "Those of you illegally occupying the Palace have one hour and ten minutes to vacate the premises...or we will forcibly remove you! I repeat, we will forcibly remove you at five o'clock"

He told Ruben and Larry to wait out front with Antonio and then banged on the heavy doors of the Palace. "It's Fernando Lopez again," he shouted. "I'm here to talk with Henry."

The doors opened a crack, just enough to allow passage. Inside, he saw the mess that had resulted from the two-day occupation: garbage, bottles, food containers, blankets and pillows for the sleeping warriors, all piled up in the front rooms and in the courtyard. Henry came out of one of the back rooms looking like he hadn't slept in a week. Unshaven, with dark circles below his eyes, and wearing a holster now, Henry nodded and motioned for him to follow. He led him into the gift shop where there was a tiny office.

Henry pointed to a chair. "Sit."

"Henry, you look exhausted."

"It's true, I'm too old for this kind of thing."

He looked around, noticing that several of Henry's followers also carried weapons. The sight disheartened him. Had all of them lost their minds?

"I thought you were going to make peace," Henry said, challenging him. "Instead you've brought back the Caballeros."

"No, they're a bunch of young punks calling themselves the Cavalier Club. They have nothing to do with the Caballeros. We'll take care of them. For that I give you my word."

"Then why are you here?"

"Ruben's outside. He agrees to the cease fire. He'll abide by the agreement to eliminate the Entrada from Fiesta. He wants you to call off the occupation and come out first. Then the two of you can shake hands and be done with this whole misunderstanding."

"What do you mean by misunderstanding?"

He explained again why Tito was murdered and that it had nothing to do with the Entrada.

Henry listened closely to his explanation. He shook his head sadly at the mention of young girls being sex-trafficked. Finally he raised his hand and said, "No more."

"Sure, I just want you to understand why Tito was murdered."

"Okay...I will agree to the cease fire, if Ruben is serious. Let me tell my people. Then you and I can go outside to make peace."

He waited while Henry went off to tell his warriors the news. They were scattered around the Palace, guarding back doors and windows and watching for possible attempts to storm the museum.

When Henry returned, his people followed behind him. His supporters now numbered well over thirty.

Henry removed his holster and handed it to the woman at the door. Then he turned to him. "Okay then, let's do this. I think it's a good day to make peace."

The woman stationed at the entrance threw open the heavy doors, revealing the armed punks gathered on the grandstand and a small but growing crowd of onlookers on the Plaza. He stepped outside first, keeping an eye on Ricky Lucero as he did so. Henry followed cautiously, as if he didn't trust Ruben and his posse to keep their part of the agreement. Behind Henry came two of his supporters serving as bodyguards. Both of them had left their weapons inside. They positioned themselves off to the side, joining Larry Aragon.

He brought the two leaders together, his hands on their backs. "Okay. Here's the agreement. Ruben, you and the Caballeros agree to abide by the decision to eliminate the Entrada permanently from Fiesta; and Henry, you and your followers agree to leave and never again occupy the Palace of the Governors. Now shake hands. I'll have an official document for you both to sign later."

The two men shook hands and then exchanged a few friendly words.

Suddenly a shot rang out from the Plaza, ricocheting off the stucco on the side of the Palace of the Governors a few inches above Henry's head. Everyone under the portico hit the ground, including Ruben and

Henry, Fernando and Larry. Everyone except Antonio, who sprinted across the street, bounded onto the bandstand, and backhanded Ricky Lucero with such force that he was knocked off the bandstand onto the stone sidewalk. Enraged, Antonio pounced on the helpless Lucero, picked him up by his collar, and slammed him repeatedly against the metal railing of the bandstand.

Lucero screamed, bawling like a baby, while Antonio cursed and threatened to break him over his knee.

He rushed over to restrain Antonio, who he'd never seen so angry. "Easy, Antonio. Don't kill him!"

"What?" Antonio muttered, his eyes glazed.

"Easy...take it easy, everyone's okay, everything's under control."

He spotted Manny walking across Palace and waved him over.

"Manny, you and Antonio take the kid back to the station and book him for negligent use of a deadly weapon or attempted murder or whatever you want, just don't hurt him, okay?"

"Will do," Manny said, eyeing Antonio.

Antonio's bright red face looked like it was about to explode. Growling, he loosened his grip around the young man's neck and shook him like a rag doll before letting go.

The kid slid down on the sidewalk as though he didn't have a bone in his bruised and battered body.

Lucero's friends, the other teenagers who called themselves the Cavaliers, quickly put away their weapons and shrank back, horrified both at what Lucero had done and what Antonio had done to Lucero.

It took a few minutes for Antonio to regain his composure. When he did, he said, "Let's go, kid." He pulled Lucero up by his long greasy hair and pushed the sobbing kid ahead of him. He kept pushing him down Palace to Washington and around to the station. Manny followed to make sure Antonio didn't inflict any more physical damage on the kid.

Meanwhile, he climbed up on the bandstand where the cowering members of the Cavalier Club watched Antonio herd their cowardly leader away without even bothering to use handcuffs. He impounded Lucero's AR-15 for evidence and then turned to deal with the others.

"Okay, kids, I'll give you one minute to get the hell out of here.

If you don't, I'll arrest all of you. Even better, I'll put you in custody of Antonio there. He has a way of getting through to people like you."

The young men scurried off without looking back.

"Show's over," he said to the crowd of gawkers on the Plaza. "Move along."

Henry and Ruben were talking under the portico. He stopped to thank both of them for making peace. "Despite all the trouble we've had getting here, Tito would be happy to see this."

Then he took the impounded AR-15 and hurried to the station to deal with what was left of young Ricky Lucero.

24
Saturday

When Tommy didn't answer his phone the next morning, he decided to pay him a visit. So he drove over to Tommy's apartment on Don Gaspar and found Pete Rodriguez parked outside in his cruiser, offering protection. He parked in the street and walked up to the cruiser. Pete rolled down his driver's window and greeted him with a smile and a thumbs up.

"Any problems?"

Pete smiled. "No, not really. Guy in a Range Rover drove by a couple of times yesterday but didn't stop. Could have been the guy you mentioned seeing at Buffalo Thunder."

"Was it blue and white?"

"Yeah, and the guy was driving real slow, like he was checking out the place."

"Okay. Good work. If he stops, be careful. Don't take any chances."

He walked to the door of Tommy's apartment and knocked. When there was no answer he knocked again more firmly. Finally the door opened a crack revealing a sleepy, bare chested Baca in pajama bottoms staring at him. "Oh, Fernando...come on in," he said, opening the door wide. "You should have called before coming over."

"I did. You didn't answer." He walked past Tommy into the small apartment.

"I guess I must have turned the sound off."

He stopped when he saw Ana, totally naked and sprawled on a bed in the back bedroom. A white sheet twisted around her sleeping body, with one long leg and her pointed breasts visible from where he was standing. Tommy had left the bedroom door wide open.

"I see you two are on friendly terms."

Tommy blushed. "We decided to follow your suggestion and get married. That way she can get a green card and eventually become a U.S. citizen. Then she won't have to go back to Sinaloa. Both her parents were murdered by the drug cartel. She came across the border legally at Aqua Prieta. When Warner's agents recruited her, she managed to keep a copy of her birth certificate along with her visa, so we're going to do it. Hopefully make her legal."

"Wait, I only suggested you tell the sheriff you're getting married. I did not suggest you actually get married."

"Yeah, but the more we thought about what you said, the more it made sense to actually do it. You know what I mean?"

"Are you sure she's not just using you to get legal status?"

Baca laughed. "No, I'm not even sure of my own motivation. I might be using her!"

"Well, it's your business. I just need to ask Ana a couple of questions about the ranch. It's very important, because the other young women there seem to have disappeared."

"Oh, okay, let me wake her up. Have a seat," he said, motioning to a chair in the front living room.

He took a seat and waited. A few minutes later they came in, Tommy wearing a T-shirt and jeans and Ana in a long robe. They both looked happy and sat on the sofa across from him.

"Sorry to bother you this early, Ana, but we need your help again. We went out to the ranch with a search warrant yesterday morning and were surprised to find all the girls gone. They'd completely disappeared. The barracks building looked empty, with no trace of anyone ever living there. Do you have any idea what could have happened to the girls? Could Robert Warner have taken them to another nearby location? Or another of his ranches maybe?"

She shook her head. "No, they still there. He have what he call a Japanese tea- house where he hide them. It's right on the river there under some trees, not too far away. He took us there once with blindfolds, so we don't know the way. But it's over a small rise, maybe a ten-minute walk. We have cots there and a campfire to cook, but no running water, no toilet."

He shook his head. "Even the chests of drawers and the cabinets in the bathroom were empty."

"Yeah, because they put everything in garbage bags and take it away, bring it to the tea-house."

"So it's like a camp? On the Galisteo River?"

"Si. We stay there a day, maybe two, and then he bring us back to the ranch for business."

"No wonder we couldn't find anything," he said, mostly to himself.

"And if you scream or try to make noise, they beat you. They kill one girl who try to run back to ranch screaming. Strangle her to death and then bury her in a graveyard there."

"A graveyard?"

"Si, a small graveyard, maybe two or three graves. The graves no have names. It's sacrilegious, a sin I think."

His first thought was A. J. Hoke. Would they find his body there? Who else might be buried at Three-Hills Ranch?

He smiled. "Thanks, Ana, this really helps. One more question. What's Joan Novak's role at the ranch? Is she a psychiatrist?"

Ana laughed, tossing her long black hair to the side. "No, she's nurse. She help with hygiene and medication. She gets girls ready for sex, fixes their hair, and gives them lots of pills to make them sedated."

"The girls are sedated before sex?"

Ana nodded. "Always. To keep them passive and obedient. So rich men can do what they want with them and no fight back."

Here Tommy stood up. "Damn! Do we have to go into the details? I think you get the gist of what's been going on at the ranch, Fernando."

"Sorry, Tommy, I didn't mean to offend you—or Ana. "I think I have all the information I need."

Before leaving, he took Tommy outside on the porch. "Listen, be careful until we can get these people behind bars. Don't go anywhere without protection. They're likely to come after Ana again, because she's our main witness at the moment. She can put them all behind bars, and they know it. They'll do anything to stop her. Do you understand?"

Tommy nodded.

"Call me if you need help, day or night."

Tommy stood on the porch watching him walk away and then

went back inside and locked the door behind him.

He drove back downtown. He hurried into the station ignoring Linda at the front counter who claimed to have a message for him. He went directly to his office, sat down at his desk, and called Jodie on her cell.

"I know where the girls are!" he said when she picked up the phone. "I talked to Ana, and she told me where they hide the girls when they want to keep them out of sight."

"Where?"

"Can you come down to the station? We need to make a plan."

"I'm on my way," she said and hung up the phone.

25

They arrived at Noon. They parked behind an outcropping of rock on Hoke's property where the cruisers would be out of sight to anyone coming in or out of Three-Hills Ranch. Jodie again brought John Rodriguez, and he brought Antonio and Hank Dixon, a member of the SFPD Swat Team and a registered sharpshooter. Hank lugged an old but trusty 308 Winchester on his back. Old and grizzled, Hank could still outshoot anyone on the force. These days he spent most of his time on a shooting range since there wasn't much call for a sharpshooter in a city as upscale as Santa Fe.

The rest of them packed their service revolvers and wore bulletproof vests over their uniforms.

"Let's spread out and walk in single file," he said.

He took the lead, walking along the dry riverbed, followed by Jodie and John and Antonio, with Hank bringing up the rear. They followed the Galisteo River as it circled around behind the three hills that cradled the ranch. The soft white sand made for slow going, especially for Hank carrying his heavy rifle. The further they went, the thicker the sumac and saltbush growing on the banks.

Around one bend they came across a grisly sight: a scattering of deer carcasses slaughtered crossing the riverbank. The badly decomposing carcasses swarmed with flies and maggots and stunk to high heaven. They covered their noses and avoided the area by walking through the bushes on the riverbank.

Moments later he nearly stepped on a trove of bleached white bones. At first he thought he'd found a human rib cage, but on closer examination the white bones turned out to be from a small deer, a young doe probably. Still, he and the others avoided stepping on the bones out of respect or superstition or whatever. All this death could only be a bad omen.

Apparently Warner's gunmen considered any animal on four legs fair game for target practice.

He had no idea how far they'd walked when they finally saw a stand of tall cottonwood trees up ahead. The trees spread their gnarled branches and green leaves over the river, clearly fed by an underground spring. On the opposite side of the riverbank from the trees a red sandstone cliff marked a bend in the river. At the very top of the cliff a small open-air platform that looked like a duck or deer blind commanded the approach to the cottonwood grove. The platform's high perch reminded him of a prison guard tower.

He motioned for everyone to stop. He took out his binoculars and surveyed the area. He saw the outlines of a hexagonal wooden structure concealed under a tangle of cottonwood branches, their leaves just starting to turn yellow. Unless you knew what you were looking for, you would never notice the hidden structure. The so-called Japanese tea-house had screens instead of windows on all six of its sides. Its open sides would make it more or less a summer house, only usable during the warm months. In Winter it would be like living in a freezer.

A wooden deck jutted out from the front of the tea-house and extended over part of the riverbed, directly across from the platform, which was a good ten feet higher than the deck.

While scanning with his binoculars he noticed movement on the high platform. Instinctively he jumped to the side just as a flash of light erupted from the tree branches.

Crack!

Sand kicked up beside him.

"Get down!" Jodie screamed.

Behind him Hank quickly moved to the edge of the riverbank and placed his 308 Winchester on its tripod. It took him only seconds to locate the shooter, aim, and return fire. The first bullet splintered the wooden railing and sent pieces of wood exploding into the air like shrapnel.

Crack! came another shot from the platform.

The bullet zinged over his head and exploded in the sand somewhere behind him.

Hank lifted his tripod and carried it forward a few paces and up the bank on higher ground to get a better view.

Crack! again from the platform.

He heard a muffled thud behind him.

Hank fired again. This time they heard a deep groan and then silence from the platform. When he looked with his binoculars, he saw the shooter's arms dangling over the wooden railing. The shooter was down.

He started for the platform when he heard Jodie scream behind him.

"Shit! John's been hit!"

He raced back to help John, who lay flat on his back with a confused look on his face. Not wasting any time, he ripped open John's vest with both hands looking for the wound.

"Where is it?" Jodie asked.

He located a gaping hole in the lower portion of the bulletproof vest. He cursed when he realized the bullet had penetrated the vest. He tore John's shirt open at the bottom and found a small, blackened hole in his lower left abdomen. The slug had ripped through the shirt and lodged just beneath the skin. An ugly black circle surrounded the wound.

"Here, let me in there."

Jodie took a small first aid kit from her belt and opened a gauze pad, which she pressed against the wound. "John, can you understand me? Keep pressure on the pad. It's a small flesh wound, you're going to be fine. Okay?"

John looked at her and nodded.

She placed a second gauze pad over the wound and then ripped off several lengths of white medical tape and taped them over the pad. "Just keep pressure on the pad, John. It's just a flesh wound. We'll be back for you, okay?"

Again he nodded.

"Let's finish the job."

Jodie stood up and moved forward. Everyone followed.

They spread out as they approached the tea-house. He and Antonio went around to the front toward the platform, while Jodie and Hank went back behind the house. Hank set up his tripod on the riverbank directly behind the tea-house to provide cover for Jodie.

He led the way down the arroyo to the front of the structure. He climbed a series of steps up to the top of the wooden platform, weapon in hand. He found the shooter slumped over the railing, the Barrett wedged under his body and his arms dangling into empty space. Like the others, he wore a khaki uniform. His cap had fallen into the riverbed.

Moving closer, he noticed the exit wound on the back of the man's shirt and didn't bother to check for a pulse. Hank's Winchester did nearly as much damage as the Barrett.

Climbing down, he heard Antonio shouting below.

"Drop the gun! Now!" One of Warner's men had stepped out of the tea-house only to find himself staring down the barrel of Antonio's Smith & Wessen.

The man froze, like a deer caught in the headlights of a car. He glanced nervously at Antonio and then at him. Finally he dropped his gun with a loud clatter on the wooden deck.

Antonio pounced, not wasting any time. He spun the man around, shoved him against the wall, cuffed him, and then kicked his legs out from under him. The man fell heavily on the deck.

He joined Antonio on the porch. "Good work."

Just then someone screamed inside the tea-house.

Moments later another man dressed in khaki stepped out of the tea-house with one of the young girls as a hostage. He held the frightened girl in front of him, a revolver pressed against the back of her head. She was crying and whimpering, trying not to stumble as he pushed her forward on the wooden deck.

"Drop your guns!" the man barked.

He and Antonio placed their weapons on the deck.

"Now stand back!" the man said. "You make a move and I'll blow her brains out! Get out of my way!"

Enraged at the sight of the young girl, who couldn't have been more than thirteen or fourteen years old, he fought his urge to rush the man and beat his brains out right there on the porch.

"Take it easy. Don't hurt her," Antonio said, strangely more composed than him.

The man pushed the girl forward, step by step, moving toward the stairway down to the trail that would take them back to the ranch.

He and Antonio stood back, out of the way.

Before the gunman could reach the stairway Jodie stepped out of the tea-house and crept up behind him. She pressed her revolver against the back of his head and said, "You're a dead man."

The man froze, not knowing what to do. "Okay, don't shoot me. I'll drop my gun."

As soon as his gun hit the floor, Antonio grabbed him by the shoulders and spun him around.

"Let me have the honor," he said, stepping forward. He cuffed the man and then gave him a hard shove into the railing followed by a swift kick in the ass that sent him sprawling on the deck.

Jodie motioned them over. "Wait until you see this."

They followed her inside the tea-house where three other young women huddled together on a wooden bench built into the wall. They held on to one another for dear life, too frightened to speak. All wore identical shorts and halter tops.

"They're frightened out of their minds. The bastards who did this will pay—one way or another. I gave them my word."

"It's not over yet." He waved to Hank, motioning for him to join them at the tea-house.

On the way up Hank stopped to look at something behind the structure. Then he called to him. "Fernando, you need to come check this out. Looks like there might be some graves down here."

Graves? He remembered what Ana had said about the graveyard.

He climbed down the hill to take a look. Off to the side of the riverbank he saw three mounds, each with a round stone on top. One of the mounds appeared to be freshly dug.

The sight of the unmarked graves depressed him. He felt his heavy load getting heavier. He suspected the worst: that he would have to tell Mrs. Hoke her husband had been murdered.

"A. J. Hoke," Antonio said, coming up behind him.

"That would be my guess. The other two, who knows?"

After they walked back to the deck, he turned to Hank. "Keep an eye on these two until we get back, okay? You don't have to worry about the fellow up there on the platform."

Hank smiled.

"Let's go get Warner," he said, noticing Jodie already walking up the trail to the ranch.

26

He and Antonio followed Jodie over the small rise to the ranch. She marched like a woman possessed. He wished she would slow down and wait for them because the Foreman had yet to be accounted for. He considered the Foreman the most dangerous of Warner's gunmen now that the sniper had been killed. When they entered the yard they found the ranch eerily quiet, with no sign of activity anywhere. It looked like a scene from a science fiction movie where all life in a city had vanished overnight, leaving a ghost town.

"Let's start with the house," Jodie said, pointing the way.

They walked through the garden up to the front door. Jodie didn't bother to knock. She opened the door wide and stepped inside the foyer and then hesitated when she heard the sound of sobbing. Looking around, she saw Joan Novak sitting in the front room weeping uncontrollably, with her face buried in her hands. Jodie motioned for him and Antonio to remain behind while she went ahead to check on the distraught Novak.

"What's happened? Why are you crying?"

Novak looked up at Jodie and brushed the short blond hair out of her eyes, still sobbing. The tall thin woman looked even more emaciated than the last time they'd seen her. "I'm so sorry...I was just trying to help the girls...to take care of them as best I could...to keep them safe from him and his friends...he's a monster...when he asked me, I had no idea what he'd be doing with them...I swear, I only agreed to come as their nurse...to take care of them...I had no idea."

For a moment Jodie was taken aback, not knowing what to say.

"Well, tell that to the District Attorney. If what you say is true, he's likely to cut a plea deal with you for your testimony against Warner and the others. He'll need you as a witness."

Novak continued to weep. "I thought I could help...take care of the girls...so he wouldn't hurt them."

"Where are they?" he asked from a distance. "Where's Warner and the Foreman now?"

"I don't know," Novak sobbed. "They were with two of the girls. I don't know where they took them."

"Fuck!" Jodie said, turning to him. 'I'll check out the barracks, and you guys go through the house."

He watched Jodie run out of the house before turning back to Novak. "You stay right here until we get back, okay?"

She nodded.

He grabbed Antonio's arm. "You take the left wing, and I'll take the right."

He hurried down the hallway, checking each of the rooms as he proceeded: study, gym, media room. No sign of Warner or the Foreman. He turned the corner to the south wing where all the bedrooms were located. He checked the first two bedrooms with the garish red décor and the heart-shaped beds.

All of a sudden he noticed a door slightly ajar on the courtyard side of the hallway. He stepped through the door into a small room with an elevator off to one side. An elevator to the basement! He wondered why he hadn't thought of this earlier. It was too late to worry about that now, though. Guarding the elevator stood the Foreman. He did not look happy to have a visitor.

"Get out of here!" the Foreman barked, fists closed tight. "This is private property."

"So you keep telling me."

"You have no right to be here."

"Wrong again."

The Foreman stared at him, his face twisted with anger. He sputtered, trying to form words.

"You're under arrest for kidnapping and sex trafficking and whatever else the District Attorney decides to prosecute you for. We have two of your buddies handcuffed on their bellies over at the tea-house, and your sharp shooter is dead. You're all alone now, pal. Warner doesn't give a damn about you. You're nothing but a hired hand to him."

"Fuck you!"

"Make it easy on yourself. If you surrender now, and testify against Warner, the District Attorney will cut you some slack. I'll talk to the D.A. I'll help you as much as I can. Warner's the sex trafficker, not you. He's the big man. He's the one we want. What do you say?"

The Foreman considered for a split second and then shook his head. He reached for his holster, but then changed his mind. Instead, he pulled out a switchblade knife and opened the blade.

"You're making a big mistake," he said, as the heavily muscled Foreman moved ominously closer.

He reached for his revolver just as the Foreman lashed out with a karate kick. The gun clattered to the floor.

Before he could move away the Foreman kicked him in the gut, doubling him over. He sunk down on his ass, gasping for breath.

The Foreman smiled. "Just you and me now, no one to help you out."

Just as he said that the door slammed open against the wall and Antonio stepped into the room. He surveyed the situation quickly and then turned to the Foreman. "Put the knife down."

"Why don't you make me, tough guy," he said, laughing. The bigger they come, the harder they fall."

Antonio reached down to give him a helping hand. When he did, the Foreman sucker punched him in the jaw, sending him careening into the wall.

Antonio stood up straight rubbing his jaw, fire in his eyes. The Foreman seized the moment to duck out the door, still brandishing his knife. Antonio followed in hot pursuit.

On his hands and knees now, he crawled over to the door and watched the battle. The Foreman made it halfway down the hall before Antonio tackled him from behind. The knife shot across the floor into the wall. The Foreman elbowed Antonio in the face, driving the big ex-Marine off momentarily. But Antonio grabbed the Foreman's leg as he tried to run off, pitching him face down on the floor. Both men hurled curses at each other.

On their feet now the two men faced off like boxers, sizing each other up. The Foreman struck first with a hard right hand, backing Antonio up. But as the Foreman moved forward, Antonio caught him with a vicious left uppercut to the chin that snapped the Foreman's head back. Antonio followed that with a straight right hand that dropped the Foreman to his knees.

Desperate, the Foreman reached for his holster, but before his hand could remove the revolver Antonio kicked him hard in the face, sending him crashing backwards on the floor, his nose spurting blood. The Foreman made one more attempt to reach his gun, but before he could Antonio rushed over and blocked him, kicking the gun out of his reach. Then Antonio stomped down hard on the outstretched arm, snapping bones. The Foreman screamed in pain.

Antonio smiled, looking down at the screaming man. "Doesn't matter how small, they all fall," he taunted the Foreman.

Antonio deftly flipped the Foreman on his stomach and cuffed his hands behind his back, listening to the sound of the wounded man sputtering and choking on his own blood.

Antonio grunted at him when he came hobbling down the hallway to pick up the Foreman's knife and gun.

"You better turn him over on his back," he said. "You don't want him to choke to death."

"I don't?"

He tried to laugh but his ribs ached too much.

"He'll be okay, he's a tough sonofabitch," Antonio said.

"So I noticed. I don't think I've seen anyone give you that much trouble—ever."

"He packed a good punch."

"Not good enough."

Antonio smiled.

"Okay, let's finish this. We have one more to round up," he said.

They walked back to the elevator, not knowing what they would find on the lower level. "Are you ready?"

"Let's roll."

They rode the elevator down, a slow, silent ride that seemed to last forever. When the door opened they found themselves in a small hallway with one door at the far end. A secret room.

He tried the door but found it locked. So he made room for Antonio, who raised his huge right leg and smashed in the door with one kick. They heard screams and confusion from across the room. The low lighting bathed the room in a sickly red glow, illuminating an enormous heart-shaped bed on which two young girls struggled to free themselves. When they managed to claw their way out from under the sheets, they stood frozen in the red light, with tiny pointed breasts and little tufts of pubic hair. Frightened children.

Enraged by the sight of the frightened, quivering girls, he rushed to the bed and ripped off the sheets. He wrapped each of the young girls in a sheet and then turned to face Robert Warner.

Warner seemed to be confused about what was happening in the room. He climbed out on the other side of the bed and stood there totally naked, with his erection wilting like a balloon losing its air. His entire body from the neck down was covered with thick black hair, making him look like some lascivious satyr out of Greek Mythology, a beast with an enormous sexual appetite that preyed on young women indiscriminately and by force.

"You filthy—" Antonio started to say but never bothered to finish. Instead he rushed Warner, grabbing the naked man by the throat and slamming him back against the wall. Warner's head rattled on the concrete wall.

"Don't hurt him, Antonio!" he shouted, afraid the big man would kill Warner.

Antonio turned to look at him with angry eyes. "Why not?"

"Because I want him to spend the rest of his life in jail. I want him to pay for what he's done to these girls."

Antonio released Warner, who slumped down on the bed babbling and talking to himself.

"Why don't you take the girls up to the lobby and ask Novak for help. She claims that's why she's here—to help the girls. Maybe she can find some clothes for them."

Antonio nodded, glancing at Warner. "Okay." He motioned for the two girls to follow him, gently taking their arms and leading them out of the room. The girls, still quivering, went with Antonio.

He listened to the elevator doors close and then the sound of wheels and pulleys grinding as the elevator slowly rose to the top floor. He found himself alone with Warner. Part of him wanted to shoot the pedophile and then claim self-defense. One bullet would rid the world of the scum and make certain he could never prey on young girls again. One bullet would eliminate the possibility that all Warner's money and lawyers could get him off and allow him the freedom to continue abusing young girls. He'd become accustomed to rich people like Warner finessing the legal system to get out of even the most serious charges. He didn't want that to happen here, not with someone as filthy as Warner.

But another part of him resisted the temptation of a quick, easy resolution. He had a job to do. And they had the goods on Warner, more than enough evidence to convict him. Warner would suffer more in jail than he would from a bullet in the head. He would be locked up with gangbangers and murderers who would make him pay for his crimes every day of his incarceration. Warner had earned his place in hell.

Okay, let's go, Warner. You're under arrest for murder, for sex trafficking, and for having sexual relations with minors. You're going to spend the rest of your life in jail."

Cowering, Warner began to babble in a child's voice. "What? What's going to happen to Bobby? Bobby can't go to jail...no, not Bobby. You can't do that to Bobby."

He walked over and slapped Warner hard across the face.

Warner seemed to wake up out of some sort of spell or paroxysm.

"Let's go."

Warner looked down at his naked crotch. "Oh...okay. Give me a few minutes to get dressed. I'll be right up. Do this one thing for me so I can preserve some shred of dignity. I don't want to be naked. Please."

"All right, but hurry up. I'll be waiting for you upstairs at the elevator."

Riding the elevator he realized he'd made a mistake by not checking the room for a weapon. He remembered a bedside table and cabinets along the far wall. Warner just might have a gun hidden away in one of the drawers. He debated whether he should go back down. In the end he decided to leave it alone. If Warner had a gun and could muster enough courage to take his own life...well, it would save everyone a lot of trouble. Or so he rationalized.

Three, four minutes later he began to have second thoughts about leaving Warner unsupervised. Finally he decided to go back down. He rode the elevator down to the basement and opened the door. Shocked, he stood in the doorway looking at an empty room. He cursed himself for being so cavalier.

Warner had escaped!

27

Beginning to panic, he quickly looked under the bed and in the closet but found no sign of Warner in either place. He looked around for other possibilities. There were no other visible exits, but he saw a bedside table, a massage table, and a soft loveseat on which satyr Warner could fuck his prey while sitting upright if the bed became too boring.

Then he noticed a chest of drawers built into the rear wall, including what looked like a broom closet. He walked over to the narrow closet door and opened it. He found himself looking into a long, narrow tunnel. So Warner had an escape route planned all along! He entered the underground tunnel and walked a few paces until he saw daylight up ahead, at which point he turned around and ran back into the house to alert Antonio and Jodie.

Once again the elevator seemed to take forever. The wheels and pulleys moved incrementally, centimeter by centimeter.

When the doors finally opened he ran out of the elevator yelling for Antonio. He found him outside coming back from accompanying Novak and the two young girls to the barracks to find clothing for the girls.

Antonio waved, not understanding.

"Warner's escaped!" he shouted. "He had an escape tunnel in the bedroom! He's gone!"

Antonio ran toward the house, meeting him half way. "What the fuck? How could you have let him escape?"

He never had a chance to explain.

Up on the trail leading to the tea-house they heard Jodie shouting at them. She pointed toward the helicopter pad. "Hurry up!" she shouted. "He's escaping! He's up here!"

Jodie ran toward the helicopter pad, while he and Antonio lagged behind. They ran up the hill to where the trail to the tea-house veered to the left and circled around behind the house to the helipad. From about fifty yards away they could see that Warner had already reached the copter and was attempting to start the engine, the blades beginning to churn.

Jodie reached the stairway up to the helipad just as the copter began to lift off. She took out her service revolver and waved it at Warner, ordering him to stop. Suddenly she was engulfed in a windstorm that churned up dust and dead brush from the hillside. Partially blinded, she shot at the helicopter once and then again, hearing the ping of the bullets striking the metal.

She kept firing, blinded by the dust, until she had to turn away and cover her face with her arm.

Lifting off, Warner took his eyes off the instrument panel for just an instant and looked down at Jodie. In that instant the copter rolled to the right, its blades just grazing the side of the hill behind the pad. The copter spun out of control. It somersaulted grotesquely and then crashed into the hillside, bursting into flames. Suddenly the machine exploded, sending fragments hurtling through the air and then when they reached their zenith slowly falling to the ground in slow motion. The fragments, some flaming and some burned black, showered the area with twisted, smoking metal that stank of burning fuel and electronics.

Jodie stumbled back down the hill, coughing from the acrid smell. "Get back! The smoke is toxic!" she shouted at them. She bent over, hands on her knees, struggling for air.

They waited for her at the bottom of the hill until she finally came weaving down the trail coughing. From a distance the three of them watched the fragments flame and then burn out on the hillside. Some of the dried grasses on the hill began to smolder, threatening to burst into a full-blown grass fire.

He turned to Antonio. "Call the Galisteo Fire Department and have them send out a truck. If the wind picks up, we could be in trouble."

"Okay...and I saw a couple of fire extinguishers in the house. You want me to get them?"

"Yes, good idea."

While Antonio went to make the call and fetch the fire extinguishers, he called Linda back at the station and told her to send a medevac out for John and a police van for the six girls and Novak.

"Got it," Linda said.

"Wait, I'm not done yet. I also need you to send out a forensic team for two deceased individuals and three unmarked graves."

"Jesus, Fernando! You're asking me to send out a caravan! What have you been doing out there?"

"My job." He ended the call before she could respond with one of her wisecracks.

He knew the graves would have to be cordoned off and exhumed one at a time, which would take a couple of days. He doubted forensics would start digging before Monday morning. They wouldn't know if one of the three graves contained Hoke's remains until late Monday or even Tuesday. That meant he might not have to break the news to Mrs. Hoke until Tuesday at the earliest. He wasn't looking forward to that, his least favorite part of the job.

Jodie came up to him. "What about the Foreman and the other two we have handcuffed back at the tea-house?"

"Antonio and I want the pleasure of escorting the Foreman. And we'll take one of the other two."

Jodie nodded. "I can take the other one."

"We'll book them at the station and hold them for the weekend at least. Then we'll just have to hope the damn judge doesn't release them on bond."

While they waited, they saw Antonio coming around the house lugging two heavy fire extinguishers. He dropped them on the gravel trail.

"Let's start with the helipad. We'll need to put out anything burning on or around the concrete so the medevac can land to pick up John. The copter should be here in a few minutes."

So he and Antonio hoisted up the industrial fire extinguishers and struggled up the hill. The smoke and the smell had died down somewhat. They sprayed the entire area around the helipad, snuffing out any trace of fire or smoke and removing any debris that would prevent the medevac from landing. When they finished, the helipad was totally clear.

Then they started up the hill spraying the larger fragments, which were still smoldering. The cabin had exploded into a hundred pieces of smashed, twisted metal. Bits and pieces of the blades littered the hill from top to bottom.

"What's this?" Antonio asked, setting down his fire extinguisher.

He came over to take a look. What he saw looked at first like a burned log. Then he realized they had found the blackened remains of Robert Warner, missing one leg and one arm. The remains resembled an incinerated hunk of meat pulled out of the charcoals of some barbecue. Smoke exuded from the charred, blistered body like the proverbial soul escaping mortal flesh.

He looked away in disgust. "None other than Robert Warner Esquire. Wait until forensics see this."

Antonio agreed. "Not a job I'd want."

By the time the Galisteo Fire Department arrived they had extinguished all the flames on the hill. The big pumper truck roared up the gravel road into the ranch and then screeched to a stop behind the house. One of the firefighters jumped out of the truck and ran up to them.

"Where's the fire?" he asked, a heavy-set man wearing overalls and a red fire helmet. Then he saw the smoking remains of the helicopter on the hill. "What happened there?"

"Pilot lost control. The copter burst into flames when it hit the hill."

"Shit! Doesn't look like there's much left."

"We're worried about a grass fire."

"Yeah, it's a tinderbox out here. We'll get the hose."

They backed the pumper truck slowly toward the helipad, until they couldn't squeeze in any further. Using their own supply of water, two of them climbed the hill with a hose and drenched the entire hillside.

It took them less than thirty minutes to soak the hill and then put away their big hose.

As the firefighters drove off, they heard the sound of a medevac approaching. The copter circled once, dipped to acknowledge contact, and then descended slowly onto the concrete pad, staying as far away as possible from the hillside covered with burned wreckage. The blades churned up black dust and burned debris that forced them to cover their eyes and mouths. The smell alone gagged them.

Two young medics jumped out and ran over to them carrying a stretcher. They looked skeptically at the tangled mass of burned metal on the hill. "Someone survived that?" one of them asked.

He shook his head. "No, we have a deputy with a gunshot wound around back. We'll show you."

Jodie took them back to the tea-house, where the medics loaded John onto a stretcher and brought him back to the helipad. Once in the copter, John sat up and began talking. Jodie recounted what had happened at the house ending with Warner's attempted escape and death.

"Where's the Foreman?" John asked.

"He's in the house cuffed and ready for delivery to the Big House."

"Well, good riddance to him."

Minutes later the medevac rose off the helipad. After clearing the hill, it banked left and then swung northwest toward Santa Fe.

After the medevac left, the afternoon became a waiting game. They waited until mid afternoon for the police van to take the six girls and Novak to the Christus St. Vincent Emergency Room for screening and treatment. Novak continued to have bouts of uncontrolled weeping. All six of the girls looked like something out of a Dickens novel: dirty, bedraggled, drugged, and minimally clothed. Novak didn't look much better. She had no idea if any of the girls had IDs or visas. If they did have papers, she didn't know where Warner kept them.

Miguel and Teresa didn't arrive until after four o'clock, their big forensics van chugging up the driveway from the riverbed and rolling to a stop between the house and the helipad.

He showed them the location of Robert Warner's body on the hillside and then took them down the trail to the shooter's body, still hanging over the platform near the tea-house.

Miguel nodded. "Okay. Maybe we can do the two of them tonight before it gets dark."

"Sorry, there's more." He took them behind the tea-house to the three unmarked graves.

Miguel shook his head. "How many more do you have?"

"That's it. Two bodies and three graves."

Teresa checked her watch. "We'll have to come back for the graves. It's gonna be a long weekend."

He shrugged. Nothing he could do about it.

"Long week, you mean," Miguel added.

28
SUNDAY

He sat in the shade of the tea-house watching Miguel and Teresa work inside the tent they'd erected over the three unmarked graves. He'd found a folding chair in the tea-house and set it up outside where he could watch the action. He checked his watch. Half past two. He'd been watching since noon, but Miguel and Teresa had been here since early this morning. Both had complained loudly when Chief Stuart asked them to work on Sunday, but the chief would not take no for an answer.

"I want this business finished ASAP," he said. "I don't give a damn if you have to work all night!"

He knew the chief exaggerated, even though they all felt a sense of urgency to finish the investigation now that Warner was dead and the girls rescued. Even so, the case would take some time to sort out.

Miguel and Teresa didn't want him inside the tent, so he watched from afar as they meticulously removed the layers of rock and soil piled on top the bodies. One scoop of the trowel and then another, repeated over and over. Followed by the brushes. The painfully slow process took forever, requiring more patience than he could muster. He hated waiting, one of his many faults. If only he hadn't stopped smoking. A cigarette or two would make waiting almost tolerable.

He knew the process. Once fully exposed, the bodies would be photographed and carefully examined, then bagged and taken either to their morgue in Santa Fe or directly to OMI at the University of New Mexico Hospital in Albuquerque. In a case like this the office of the state medical investigator would make the final determination on cause of death.

Miguel hollered from the tent a few minutes past three. "Fernando, come take a look at this."

He walked over to the tent and looked inside at the three shallow trenches. "What is it?"

"Look, all the bodies are female. I know you were expecting Hoke's body to be here, but it's not."

Surprised, he stepped inside the tent to get a closer look. He saw the three bodies, all female and in various stages of decomposition. The body in the newest grave looked discolored and swollen. The bodies of the other two were badly decomposed and their gender barely recognizable. The waxy smell of fresh soil and mold and death hung in the air, a smell that reminded him of the catacombs he and Estelle had visited in Rome on their honeymoon a million years ago. He'd never forgotten that distinctive smell.

"Are you okay?" Teresa asked, kneeling beside the third grave and brushing a last layer of dirt from what remained of the body's face.

"Yeah, just surprised."

Miguel pointed to the newest body. "This one was clearly strangled. You can tell by the marks around her neck. The others will take some time, given their condition. We'll have to determine how long they've been here."

He noticed the deep laceration in the newest girl's neck made by a rope or, more likely, a wire. This one looked like she might be older than the other young women he'd seen at Three-Hills, maybe all of twenty years old.

Teresa stood up from her work at the third grave and wiped the sweat from her forehead. She came over to join him and Miguel. "There's no way we can finish this afternoon. We'll have to come back tomorrow morning. When we leave we'll put a tarp over the bodies and close the tent. That should keep the animals away for one night anyway."

"Since tomorrow is Monday, we might send the bodies directly to OMI," Miguel added. "Let them take over."

He nodded. "Right. Well, I guess I'll look around a bit before I leave. Maybe Hoke is buried somewhere else out on the mesa. I don't know what else to think. Or do at this point."

While Miguel and Teresa began the process of shutting down

and closing up for the day, he walked out onto the mesa. He didn't see a fence anywhere, which meant the BLM must own all the land out here. He walked over a small hill, through a stand of scraggly piñon and juniper trees.

When he saw vultures circling overhead in the distance, he didn't think anything about them at first. He assumed they circled above another of the cattle carcasses he and Antonio had encountered on Hoke's ranch. Then he realized Hoke's ranch was located a couple miles south of where he now stood. These vultures circled over an area on the mesa directly west of Warner's tea-house, maybe a half mile away.

Curious, he began walking west along an old cattle trail, marked with pods of dried cow dung. He saw animal tracks everywhere, not only cattle, but deer, coyote, bobcat, and wild horses. He knew a herd of wild horses roamed free from Placitas in the north to the Ortiz Mountains just south of Galisteo.

A late afternoon wind kicked up as he walked, gusting ahead of him. An occasional dust devil spiraled up and dissipated into the thin dry air. Nothing but sage, cactus, and dried tumbleweed on the mesa, he mused. Not a drop of water until you came to the Rio Grande, a good twenty miles west of the tea-house. Out here animals—and humans—had to travel a long way to find water.

He saw the vultures up ahead as he followed the trail, the big black birds with speckled red heads and enormous wingspans. Three of the death birds circled overhead, but even more of them gathered on the ground around their prey. When he crunched though a tangle of dried tumbleweed, the birds scattered in all directions, a black whirlwind of flapping wings.

Coming closer, the putrid smell overwhelmed him. He stopped to cover his mouth with a handkerchief when he saw the ghastly corpse sprawled on its back in the sand, with the black barrel of a shotgun flung off to its side. Hoke's eyes had been pecked out by the vultures, as had his lips and tongue. After two days in the sun, Hoke's face had dried to the color and consistency of leather, his mouth an empty black hole wide open in one last scream.

He turned away with a mixture of anger and disgust. He needed to inform Miguel and Teresa before they left for Santa Fe. They would have to add one more body to their makeshift morgue. Then he remembered the shotgun. Walking carefully around the corpse, he picked up the shotgun and opened its chamber. He found one spent twelve gauge shell in the chamber, which meant that Hoke had managed to get off one shot before they killed him.

He placed the shotgun down in the sand where he had found it. A twelve gauge would be absolutely worthless out here against Warner's sniper, who killed at great distances.

On the way back to the tea-house he thought about what he would tell Mrs. Hoke. He would have to drive out to the ranch and tell her in person, not over the phone. Something he dreaded.

Miguel and Teresa had closed up the gravesite by the time he reached the tea-house. Their orange tent had been zipped and staked tight. He flagged them down as they loaded their van, preparing to leave.

Miguel walked over to meet him on the trail. "We're taking off now, but we should be back by nine tomorrow morning. I think we should be able to finish by mid afternoon."

He conveyed the bad news. "Well, don't rush off, because I just found Hoke's body on the mesa."

Miguel sighed. "Well, hell, I take back what I said. We may not finish tomorrow at all."

"Let me show you." He led the way back to the body.

Miguel lagged behind, not terribly excited about the prospect of yet another corpse to process.

When they approached the body, he stayed back a good twenty yards and pointed the way forward.

Miguel took a surgical mask out of his back pocket and put it over his nose and mouth when he neared the grisly sight. He bent over to examine the body. "Christ! Look at the two holes in his chest!"

He kept his distance.

"I mean, his entire chest is ripped open."

"It's probably the same fifty caliber Barrett that killed Tito. And probably the same shooter."

Miguel nodded. "Okay, I'll go get another tarp and some stakes. That should keep the vultures away until tomorrow. We'll make sure to process this one first thing tomorrow morning."

"I'll stay with him while you get the tarp. It's the least I can do."

"Suit yourself."

Miguel walked off toward the tea-house. Then he stopped and turned around. "And Fernando...if I were you I wouldn't let Mrs. Hoke see the body."

He did not respond. He stood guard over Hoke's remains, watching Miguel walk back down the trail and disappear into a bruised eastern sky already darkening purple to black.

29
TUESDAY

He sat in the front row of historic Saint Francis Auditorium waiting for Tito's memorial service to begin. Delores, Tommy, and Ana sat beside him on the bench. Behind them a veritable who's who of Santa Fe had packed the great hall: the Mayor, the Chief of Police, the entire Santa Fe City Council, the Fiesta Council, the All Pueblo Council of Governors, and many of the Caballeros. Even Ruben and Henry had come to pay their last respects, although they sat on opposite sides of the auditorium.

Shortly after the appointed hour of twelve noon Tommy walked up to the podium wearing a black coat and tie. He introduced himself and welcomed everyone to a celebration of Tito's life. He began the service by quoting from Mathew 5:9. "Blessed are the peacemakers, for they will be called the children of God," he read, and then paused to reminisce about working with Tito, who had mentored him after his graduation from UNM and treated him like a son.

"Tito told me more than once that the secret to getting along with people, even people you disagree with, is listening to them," Tommy said. "Put yourself in their shoes. Try to understand their point of view. That's how he approached his work as a mediator. He would listen carefully to both sides, tell them what he thought, and then try to find common ground."

Tommy laughed. "What Tito didn't understand was that not everybody had his gift for working with people. He was one of those truly special people who could talk to anyone and draw them out, murderers on Death Row or the Archbishop of Santa Fe, it didn't matter to him. He was never judgmental. As a mediator he was an absolute master at finding common ground, a compromise that both sides could live with."

Tommy shared anecdotes of Tito working with difficult people that made the audience laugh. Then he announced he would be taking over Tito's mediation business: "I learned everything I know about conflict resolution from working with Tito over the last five years. I plan to spend the next thirty years trying my best to live up to his example."

Tommy ended his remarks by returning to Mathew 5:9: "You are the light of the world."

After Tommy, Mayor Joe Martin spoke about how important Tito had been in the deliberations to end the Entrada. "Without Tito," Martin said, "there would never have been an agreement." Ann Lewis and Henry Ortiz followed Martin and said much the same thing, praising Tito for his patience and his generosity. Finally Delores Ruiz, the last speaker, walked slowly to the podium wearing a simple black dress.

She looked around the room at all those gathered to honor her brother. "Thank you all for coming to this celebration of Tito's life. I want you to know that I'm sad today. I'm sad because my brother was taken from me before his time...and I'm sad that I wasn't closer to Tito when he was alive...that I never told him how much I loved him when I had the opportunity. Coming back here, coming back home, I realize what I've missed all these years."

She raised her hands and pointed to the colorful murals on the walls of the great hall. "Just looking at these beautiful murals that tell the story of Santa Fe reminds me of who I am and where I belong. I owe all that to Tito, who in death brought me back home."

Delores paused for a moment to wipe away a tear. She looked around the hall and scanned the audience from one side of the room to the other. "Yes, of course I'm sad, but I'm also happy today. I'm happy to know Tito had so many friends...and to hear all the good things people have said about him today. I'm proud of what Tito did for other people and of how hard he worked for peace. And I'm especially proud to be his sister."

After she finished Delores stepped down from the podium and joined him, Tommy, and Ana. None of the speakers had mentioned Ana or her relationship with Tito, whatever its nature. Now that Tito had passed, it made no sense to any of them to pursue the matter further. Better to let it go, whatever it was. The past was the past. It died with Tito.

Moments later he and Delores made their way to the front door of the auditorium to exchange condolences with the departing guests. They thanked each person who'd come to Tito's service as he or she exited the great hall. Mayor Martin gave the typical canned response on his way out the door: "Sorry for your loss." Chief Stuart only nodded at them, not even bothering to make a comment. He apologized for the chief's insensitivity, but Delores didn't seem to mind. She was smiling now and obviously relieved, having fulfilled her obligation to her brother. She'd handled the service well. So, too, had Tommy.

Next came Ann Lewis and Henry Ortiz. "Your brother was a great man," Lewis said, looking very stately in a black suit with a blue scarf tied around her neck. "He'll be missed in Santa Fe. We counted on him for so many things, both on City Council and in his work as a mediator. There's no one else in the city who could bring us together as he could. He was truly a peacemaker."

Henry Ortiz simply held Delores' hands in silence for several long seconds and then walked away.

After the last of them had gone, Delores turned to him and said, "That was hard. I'm not good at public speaking."

"You did fine."

"Well, thank you for that."

"So what are your plans now?"

"I've decided to fly back to L.A. this weekend. I'll start the retirement process and put my house on the market. As soon as it sells, which shouldn't take long in L.A., I'll be back to stay."

He nodded.

She laughed. "I'll send some of my furniture ahead, even though there's not a lot of room here with all of Tito's junk. I guess I'll have a big garage sale to clear most of it out. Except for the study. Tommy might want all the paperwork and case files, since he's going to take over the business."

"I would imagine. It's good he's continuing the business. God knows Santa Fe needs a mediator."

She laughed. "Who doesn't?"

He turned to leave.

"What do you think I should do with Tito's ashes?" she asked, bringing him back up the steps. "It's such a beautiful day, I thought I might scatter his ashes later this afternoon."

"Where?"

"Well, I thought I might scatter them in the forest behind his house. What do you think? Maybe climb the highest hill and scatter them at the very top. That way birds could pick up bits of his ashes and spread them far and wide. Plus, it would be a comfort to me, knowing there would always be some of him right there behind the house."

"I think Tito would like that."

"I think so too," she said, pausing a moment before continuing. "I've been wondering about Tito and Ana. Has she ever said anything to you about her relationship with my brother?"

He chose his words carefully. "Not much. She said she'd grown fond of him and that she'd gone with him willingly to get away from the ranch. To tell you the truth, I never really pressed her for answers. It just didn't seem relevant after...well, at this point."

She looked at him closely. "You're probably right. Tito lived a lonely life. I think a little intimacy, even late in life and under these circumstances, could only be a good thing."

30

Linda stopped him when he walked into the Washington Avenue Station. She stared at him in mock disbelief. "What's this I see? Wearing a blue blazer and a white shirt? You must be running for office or something. Let me guess. City Council? Or how about Mayor?"

He laughed. "You say that every time I put this thing on."

"Hey, you couldn't be any worse than Joe Martin."

"True, but he has two things I don't have."

"What's that?"

"Money and looks," he said. "I look like hell in front of a camera. Joe's a pretty boy."

Once in his office he removed his old sports coat and hung it in the closet where he kept it for funerals and court appearances. Otherwise, he wanted nothing to do with the damned thing, which he'd purchased at the downtown Sears back in the day when there was a downtown Sears, before the developers moved in and upscaled Santa Fe and drove out most of the natives and their stores with high taxes and big money. Big money talks, poor folks walks. Those who doubt it should come to Santa Fe and take a look at the glitter.

He rolled up his sleeves and sat down at his desk, ready to get back to work. He checked his office phone messages and found one message from Estelle about her sister coming to visit over the weekend, which alarmed him because he didn't get along with his brother-in-law, and another from Tommy thanking him for helping at the memorial service and asking him to stop by Tito's office, now his office, when he had a chance.

He didn't know exactly why, but he felt out of sorts today. Tito's memorial service had left him unsettled. Why he couldn't say. Brooding was one thing he did not do well. So he went up front and picked up the day's *Independent* and sat down at his desk to read the irritating newspaper. Everybody in the department hated the *Independent* because it consistently pimped crime news, often blaming cops for everything from not turning on their lapel cameras to mishandling evidence. He only read a newspaper when he wanted to occupy his mind and keep it from going to the dark side.

The office phone rang a few minutes later.

"Fernando, this is Jodie," came the familiar voice. "Hey, I'm in town, just finishing some errands. Could you meet me at the Great Burrito Company for an update?"

"Sure," he said, relieved to have something to do, something to take his mind off whatever was bothering him. "When can you be there?"

"Give me fifteen minutes," she said.

So he waited a few minutes and then headed down the hallway.

"Much better!" Linda cracked as he walked past. "You look much better in rolled-up shirt sleeves than you do in a blue blazer. The classic image of the working man! The voters will love it!"

"Hah! You wouldn't vote for me anyway."

Walking down Washington Avenue he spotted Jodie sitting at one of the outdoor tables at the Great Burrito Company. She had on civies today, jeans and a western shirt. She waved when she saw him approaching.

"Sorry about missing Tito's memorial service this morning," she said as he sat down at the table. "I was shopping with my partner and it took longer than I thought it would. Sharon can be a real bitch sometimes. She's never satisfied, always fussing about everything. Takes forever."

He did not respond.

She looked at him closely. "You know I like women, right?"

Though he hadn't been sure, he nodded his head anyway.

She changed the subject. "So how did Mrs. Hoke take the news? You visited her yesterday?"

"We did, Antonio and I. She's grieving, but I think she expected the worst. Her son is coming up from Socorro to help out. She wants to stay on at the farm, but she'll need help if she does."

"Maybe her son can hook her up with some aides or health care workers, whatever she needs."

"Yeah, but she lives so far out of town...I don't know."

Jodie nodded. "I stopped by to see the girls from the ranch this morning. We found them a temporary place to stay at Esperanza Women's Shelter. The hospital only kept them one night, just to check them out thoroughly. They're malnourished and exhausted, but so far none of the tests have been positive for anything serious. Four of the six do have STDs, though, which isn't surprising considering all the swinish men who abused them."

"What happens when they eventually leave Esperanza? Any chance they can get visas?"

"That's the question. None of them have papers. They come from different places in Mexico. Actually one comes from Central America. We're trying to make a case for emergency visas, claiming they were kidnapped and brought here through no fault of their own and that we need them for the criminal prosecution of their kidnappers. We'll see what happens. The Feds aren't real helpful today, as you know."

When the waitress, Terry, came to take their orders, Jodie ordered iced tea and he asked for his usual coffee with extra cream and sugar.

"So what are you hearing from the District Attorney?" she asked when the iced tea and coffee arrived.

He sat back in his chair, knowing what the District Attorney had told him wouldn't please her. It didn't please him either.

"He says the two hired guns at the tea-house are facing five to seven on charges of conspiracy and kidnapping. The Foreman maybe a bit more, seven to ten, if Joan Novak accepts the plea deal she's been offered and testifies against him, which she's apparently agreed to do. Novak will do little if any time. She's out on bail now."

"That's all fine, but what about the dead girls? These people didn't just kidnap, they murdered five teenagers!"

"I know, but he says there's not enough evidence to connect any of the murdered girls—the two found on the highway or the three buried at the tea-house—to any particular individual. That's the problem."

"So there's no justice for the girls!" she said bluntly, getting angry. "You're telling me the people who actually carried out Warner's orders and murdered these five girls are going to walk free after five years, if that?"

"That's what I'm hearing."

"I guess I shouldn't be surprised, given how the judicial system works...or doesn't work."

He ignored her comment. "It turns out the shooter on the platform who wounded John was a former Special Forces sniper with a rank of E-six named Lonnie Johnson. He served in the most recent Iraq war. Ballistics connected his Barrett rifle to the murders of both Tito and Hoke, but of course Hank killed Johnson at the tea-house. So again, no justice...or at least no legal justice."

"And Warner, the person who orchestrated everything, died in his helicopter," she shot back. "How convenient!"

"I'm afraid so."

"I blame myself for that. I thought if I fired at the helicopter, he'd set back down and then we could grab him."

"He'd still be alive if he had."

"You know what pisses me off most about this whole affair? It's not even Warner and his hired gunmen, it's all these rich white guys who flew in here just so they could fuck a teenage girl. And these guys are going to get off scot free, hundreds of them!"

He nodded.

"Yesterday I spent the morning at Three-Hills Ranch, going through Warner's office. I found his black book, I found his flight logs, computer files, you name it. Everything's all there. You might be surprised at some of the names in the files. Well-known actors from Hollywood, politicians from both parties, people you would never imagine getting caught up in a sordid business like this. Never!"

Angry, she stood up and walked around the patio to cool off.

He watched her but didn't say a word.

She seemed calmer when she returned to their table and sat down. "Sorry. I take this stuff personally."

"I understand."

"I don't know, maybe you wouldn't be surprised at the kinds of people who visited Three-Hills Ranch. It's truly depraved...and frankly pathetic! I mean, what does it say about these old bastards that they're willing to pay thousands of dollars to fuck a child? Really! Do they get some sort of perverse boost to their ego by doing this, is that what it is? Or are they truly sadistic and just like to hurt little girls? Tell me, you're a man. What's the point?"

He held up his hands, pleading his innocence. "I don't know. I just think these people are sick...and sadistic."

"And yet they're aided and abetted by a judicial system that refuses to go after them."

"Yes, you're right, I agree," he said sadly. "The pedophiles will probably get off scot free. We don't have the resources to pursue such complicated investigations and neither do you. If I took this to the District Attorney, he'd laugh at me and give me a lecture on what it takes in a case like this to establish a burden of proof. Plus these guys are filthy rich, they have high profile lawyers who can delay and obfuscate until the state either gives up or offers a plea deal just to close the case. So what chance would we have?"

"None! That's exactly what I'm saying."

"Or we could try the feds, take it to the FBI office in Albuquerque, but we'd likely get the same response: the perpetrator is dead, so move on."

Terry appeared at their table with a look of concern on her face. "You guys okay over here? You're getting kind of animated."

Jodie raised her voice. "Not really. We're talking about pedophiles and patriarchy, it's a pisser."

Terry gave them a funny look and walked back inside.

He continued, trying to find something positive to say. Something that would please her. "I tell myself that at least we stopped one pedophile and eliminated one sex trafficking ring. He's dead, and we don't have to watch his lawyers befuddle a judge and jury."

She nodded. "There's that, I suppose, but the sad fact of the matter is that there are dozens, maybe hundreds of these sex trafficking businesses across the country, especially in the Southwest. Down here the traffickers love to prey on young girls who've just come across the border. And the same perverts who frequented Three-Hills Ranch will continue to sexually abuse teenage girls at these other compounds. The filthy bastards will continue ruining the lives of young girls because the judicial system is either incapable or unwilling to go after them!"

"Sorry, I...," he started to say but then stopped, not knowing how to continue.

After a moment of silence she reached across the table and squeezed his hand. "You're a good cop, Fernando. And you're a good man. For a straight guy."

He laughed. "Thanks. I think the same of you. Maybe we'll work together again someday."

"I'm sure we will, now that I know where to go for help. We're chronically understaffed." She finished her drink and then stood up from the table.

"I'd like that. We make a good team," he said, smiling.

"Yes we do!"

He wanted to say more, but what? What did he want from her? Respect? Friendship? Or something more? He didn't know.

Before he could speak she turned abruptly and walked away.

She waved crossing the street to Palace Avenue.

He watched her disappear down Palace as a cool September wind kicked up on the empty Plaza.

Fiesta was over for another year.

Reading Guide

1. Communities across the U.S. are struggling with the question of whether to remove monuments or discontinue activities that commemorate events that certain groups find offensive. What's the downside of this so-called 'cancel culture'? What's the upside?

2. Detective Fernando Lopez serves as a peacemaker in this novel, negotiating with both sides of the Entrada issue. Is he successful? What are his strategies, his tactics? Would these be applicable to other similar situations?

3. How does Detective Lopez discover that the Entrada dispute is not why Tito Garcia was murdered? Recount the chain of events that lead Lopez to the real killers.

4. Midway through the novel a small group of Entrada supporters march in downtown Santa Fe in violation of an agreement with the city. Violence ensues. Were police tactics successful in limiting the violence? What could the police have done differently to eliminate or further limit the violence?

5. Detective Lopez learns about the young women who are being murdered south of the city from Santa Fe County Sheriff Jodie Williams. What is his initial reaction to Williams? Does his attitude toward her change in the course of the novel? Does their relationship progress from professional to personal?

6. How do Detective Lopez and Sheriff Williams figure out that Three-Hills Ranch is a sex trafficking operation?

7. Three-Hills Ranch preys on young women. Where do the young women come from? How are they lured to the ranch?

8. In Part One Tito Garcia is considered a peacemaker and a hero for his work negotiating a settlement in the Entrada dispute. He stands as a kind of moral center. How does that change when Detective Lopez learns of his involvement in Three-Hills Ranch? Does a more complicated view of morality emerge toward the end of the novel at Garcia's memorial service?

9. In spite of their shutting down Three-Hills Ranch neither Detective Lopez nor Sheriff Williams is particularly optimistic at the end. Why not?

www.ingramcontent.com/pod-product-compliance
Lightning Source LLC
Chambersburg PA
CBHW010140030826
48979CB00024B/1076
9781632934017